"I like it, the re bordello appea

Claire pursed her lips at Jason's comment. "Oh, please. There's nothing sexy about a darkroom." She searched for her supplies. "I hate it when I can't find a thing."

"Wanna bet?" Jason came up behind her.

"That I can't find anything?" She arched her neck to scan a high shelf.

His hand came around, touching her chin. He gently turned her head sideways, then eased her body around to face him. "I meant about this place being sexy." He stepped closer and kissed her lightly on the lips.

"I see what you mean," she said when the kiss was over. She tried to think of something else to say but couldn't, instead, she leaned into him and kissed him deeply.

He lifted her onto the countertop and worked a hand beneath her shirt. "This bra is just killing me."

It was her turn and she ran her fingers around his neck, then into his thick dark hair. "Well, I'm sure we can figure a way to put you out of your suffering."

Dear Reader,

Being raised in upstate New York, I spent many a cold winter evening at an ice rink watching the best college hockey players. As a kid, I used to fantasize about being called down from the stands to don my skates and score the winning goal for the home team. Well, I grew up and so did my fantasies. I began to wonder who those superior athletes really were. And even more to the point, what did they look like without all the pads and equipment? With Jason Doyle, star player for the New York Blades, I got to create my own answers. And who better to find out the intimate details than a wisecracking, independent photographer. Claire Marsden's trotted around the world more than a few times, but she's never come across the likes of Jason!

As a new member of the Temptation family, I am delighted to join the ranks of such talented storytellers and writers. Over the years, I have been an avid reader of romance fiction, and I know of no other literary genre as consistently satisfying and well written. And to me, nothing spices up a romance as much as two quick-witted protagonists who can verbally spar—in and out of bed. A sense of humor can truly be the most effective form of foreplay.

Hope you enjoy reading Jason and Claire's story—either in or out of bed!

All the best,

Tracy Kelleher

Everybody's Hero
Tracy Kelleher

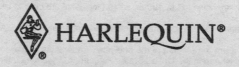

HARLEQUIN®

TORONTO • NEW YORK • LONDON
AMSTERDAM • PARIS • SYDNEY • HAMBURG
STOCKHOLM • ATHENS • TOKYO • MILAN • MADRID
PRAGUE • WARSAW • BUDAPEST • AUCKLAND

To Peter and James,
two great guys.

ISBN 0-373-69108-4

EVERYBODY'S HERO

Copyright © 2002 by Louise Handelman.

This edition published by arrangement with Harlequin Books S.A.

® and TM are trademarks of the publisher. Trademarks indicated with
® are registered in the United States Patent and Trademark Office, the
Canadian Trade Marks Office and in other countries.

Visit us at www.eHarlequin.com

Printed in U.S.A.

1

IT WAS OVER a jelly donut that Claire Marsden found the man of her dreams.

For her best friend, Trish, that is. Trish, who in high school was known as Patti with an "i."

Of course, high school had been a time of pastel turtlenecks and friendship bracelets. Now Trish was more into skimpy black knits and chunky quartz jewelry, and names ending with an "i" were definitely déclassé.

But Claire, being Claire, was not about to let her friend's sophisticated transformation pass unnoticed. Whenever she felt Trish was acting a bit uppity, she referred to her as "The Magazine Editor Formerly Known as Patti." A statement that was both annoying and true. And now that they were working together, Claire had ample opportunity to razz her friend.

Still, right now, Trish's morphing persona was the last thing on Claire's mind. In fact, she realized, it was hard to have anything on her mind, when in front of her appeared a vision of male glory that would tongue-tie even the most jaded Hollywood leading lady—with or without changing names.

Claire only hoped her cerebral shutdown was temporary. Because if she really wanted to be honest about her feelings, Jason Doyle could easily be the man of her own dreams.

After all, how many men pull up in front of Madison

Square Garden in New York City on a fire-engine-red Italian motorcycle, on time no less? But then, honesty about her own feelings was not something Claire analyzed with any great depth.

For now, she'd just enjoy the show. And thank the gods for delivering her next assignment, who, Claire was convinced, would be the perfect solution to Trish's current problems—and dreams.

Jason Doyle was also the answer to the professional hockey league's dreams. All two hundred and ten, well-proportioned pounds of him. Recently traded to the New York Blades, his aggressive style and league-leading scoring appealed to men. The women weren't immune, either, what with his devilish smile and sexy comma-shaped scar that cupped the outside corner of his right eye. The combination made him look as if he was slyly winking at some inside joke, which only he and that certain female understood. Naturally, any woman who'd ever applied lip gloss imagined herself to be that certain one.

Until now Jason had limited his commercial—and bodily exposure—to a few tasteful endorsements and a calendar to support research for children's causes. Funny how those backlighted shots of his well-oiled biceps had landed in more than a few tabloids. Or maybe not so funny, Claire reflected as she took in the way his black leather jacket hugged his broad shoulders.

Being a self-proclaimed cynic should have made her intrinsically immune to Jason's easy charm and over-the-top brand of maleness. But her cynicism appeared to have gone temporarily AWOL, especially when Jason pulled off his helmet and whipped off his mirrored sunglasses as easily as spreading cream cheese on a warm bagel. Only a fool could ignore the way her stomach did a major flip-flop, and Claire's daddy hadn't raised a fool. Jason Doyle was every bit as scrumptious; and twice as dangerous as in his photos.

Claire stiffened. That danger, coupled with that mega-powered motorcycle, signaled a personality that enjoyed living on the edge. She had had enough of that kind of life, thank you. These days, give her calm, boring consistency. Maybe a picket fence. Well, maybe not a picket fence.

But danger, or the allure of it, was just what the doctor ordered for Trish, and Claire was about to put her plan in motion. She was sure her friend would be pleased. Claire elbowed Trish. "Hubba, hubba."

"You can say that again." Trish smoothed her hands down the sides of her black leather pants. "Didn't I tell you he would make some cover story? C'mon, let's meet hockey's gift to womankind."

Claire popped the last piece of donut into her mouth and wiped the powdered sugar off the front of her ribbed sweater. "Well, it's a tough assignment, but somebody's got to do it."

Despite the ungodly hour of 6:30 a.m., a group of fans had already swarmed around Jason—no deterrent to Trish, who charged on through. "Jason, Trish Camperdown, features editor of *Focus Magazine.*"

"Ms. Camperdown, a pleasure." Jason's high-wattage smile appeared genuine. He rocked back on his heels.

Trish, normally the epitome of cool sophistication, actually giggled. He widened his smile. A full array of white teeth, large but not too large—perfect for nibbling on a girl's earlobe—practically glistened against the gray of the Manhattan skyline.

Claire was standing back a few paces, but still felt the full wattage. "You still have all your teeth." She blurted out the first thing that she thought of. Well, maybe not the first thing.

Jason looked over as if seeing Claire for the first time. He lifted his chin, surveying her closely. Not that she wasn't used to that reaction.

Men often did a double take when they first saw Claire. She wasn't beautiful, mind you; not like Trish, Claire thought. It was the fact that very few thirty-year-old women had a dramatic gray streak in their hair. She'd had it since she was eighteen, and for a time in her life had actually tried to dye it. But at the age of twenty-four or twenty-five, she had just given up, accepting it for what it was, a genetic quirk passed down by her father— a typically flamboyant quirk.

Big Jim Marsden had been a world-renowned, big-game photographer with a lust for life and a unique style all his own. If a giant rhino were charging at full speed, Big Jim could still hold a glass of bourbon in one hand and his trusty Leica camera in the other. All without flinching.

Jason Doyle didn't seem to flinch at a little sight of gray either. "I have other things intact, also," he replied.

He didn't say it with a leer. That would be cheesy, and Jason Doyle was anything but cheesy. At six foot two, with four fingers of one hand slid into the back pocket of his jeans, and his thumb looped casually on the faded denim, the man looked as solid as Mount Rushmore and radiated as much sincerity as Washington, Jefferson and Lincoln combined. He was as true blue as they came, and Claire didn't doubt that on Memorial Day he could be found in his little hometown—the guy had to come from someplace with a population of five thousand, who had wraparound porches on their white clapboard houses— placing tiny flags on the graves of the fallen war heroes.

No, when Jason Doyle said he had all his parts intact, Claire had no trouble getting the drift. It was where her imagination was drifting that had her more concerned.

"And you are?" He cocked one eyebrow and cradled his helmet against his jeans-clad hipbone.

"Claire—" An overeager fan pushed against Claire with bruising eagerness before she had a chance to finish. She bumped forward, her side landing against the hard plastic of Jason's motorcycle helmet.

He shot out a large hand, cushioning the blow. He grabbed her elbow and stopped her before her nose bumped his chin.

And what a chin. A small cleft. Early morning stubble. A slight scar along the side. That, and the one near his eye, gave him a sense of character that kept his features from being merely perfect. Claire gulped and looked up into tiger's-eye, flecked-brown eyes that spelled trouble with a capital T. "My mother warned me about guys like you," she mumbled. Claire shook her head, trying hard not to feel the sheer strength of his grip through her bulky sweater.

"That's the trouble with mothers." Jason's grin stretched wider. A devastating dimple marked one cheek. "They never look beyond the surface." Another surge of fans squashed Claire more firmly into his side.

Talk about surface. As she slammed against his body, Claire felt the energy vibrating from Jason's frame, his muscular legs straining against his worn jeans. And when she lifted her hand defensively, she felt his chest through his thin black T-shirt, his well-defined pectorals and pancake-flat stomach.

Claire shook her head. This embodiment of masculinity was meant for Trish. She should not be receiving sensory impressions with the magnitude of an air raid siren.

She raised one eyebrow, arched her neck, and gave him the slow once-over. "And a very nice surface it is, too. But there won't be much left of it if we don't get you inside."

She turned to look for Trish. Her friend's sleek chignon had come loose in the hubbub, and Claire didn't think her four-hundred-dollar Italian designer shoes could take much more of the stampede. And more fans were swarming their way. Quick action was needed. "Trish, why don't you and Jason fight your way inside? Grab one of the security guards over there to help you. We paid them overtime. They may as well earn their money."

Claire turned back to Jason. For a man about to be smothered by a band of adoring fans, he seemed remarkably calm. If anything, he was smiling more broadly than ever. "Something funny?" she asked.

"I don't think you need a mother to protect you, Claire-with-no-last-name. I think you can take care of yourself just fine."

"And something tells me you're not exactly a pushover yourself. But listen, get Trish inside. I don't think her Ferragamos can take much more of this."

"What about my bike?" He nodded sideways.

"Keys."

"Keys?"

Claire held out her hand. "I'll take the bike around the back."

Jason hesitated. "*My* mother warned me about women like you." He pulled the keys out of his pocket. "I presume you can ride one?"

"Do bears pee in the woods?" Claire waggled her fingers for him to hand over the keys.

Jason placed them in her hands. They were warm from

being next to his body. "You realize what this means, don't you?"

"I have the responsibility for a forty-thousand-dollar custom-built machine?"

"More like sixty thousand. But that's not the point. The real issue is that you now meet the first of my ten requirements for a perfect wife."

It was Claire's turn to look confused.

"Long ago, I decided that I would only marry a woman who knows how to ride a motorcycle," he said.

"Well, that's something I'm sure your adoring fans will be eager to know. But at the risk of a little too much adoration—" Claire looked over and placed Trish's hand on Jason's arm. "Trish. I think it's time you take our crowd pleaser inside."

Trish, her hairdo and her demeanor jostled by the crowd, looked only too relieved at the suggestion. Of course, a mussed coiffure on Trish simply gave her that air of just-out-of-bed chic. Her retro Persian lamb jacket hanging precariously off one shoulder and her skimpy little cashmere sweater doing the same, added to the waif-like look. "Don't worry about your bike," Trish said. She patted Jason's arm as she directed him forward. "Claire is very good with mechanical things. After a party while we were in high school, she once figured out how to circumvent the security system in my parents' house, so we could sneak in late without getting in trouble."

Jason seemed more impressed by that news than by Trish's soigné appearance. Over the crowd noise she heard, "I trust she hasn't continued this life of crime." He looked back in Claire's direction.

"I'm only tempted toward the end of the month when the paycheck's run out and the electricity bill is overdue," Claire said loud enough for him to hear.

An eager fan thrust a copy of the morning's paper and pen toward Jason to sign, and forced Claire to take a step back, giving her a better view of her gaminelike friend cozying up to hockey's hunk. And then the first thought of the morning hit her again. Here in the flesh was the answer to Trish's dreams. And while the thought should have sent her leaping with the joy and grace of a member of the Bolshoi's chorus, it was actually a little depressing. Strange. And when faced with internal confusion, Claire reacted in her instinctively glib manner. "Speaking of A-1 marriage material. You fit our bill for a fiancé."

Her voice penetrated the din of the crowd. And Jason, who had started to turn into the building with Trish leading the way, turned his head back at the sound of Claire's voice.

She smiled. For once, the calm assurance that naturally embued his features, seemed to flicker.

"Don't worry. It's for Trish, not for me," she called.

2

BY THE TIME Claire stowed the bike around the back of the arena, leaving it under the envious eye of a security guard, the rest of the contingent from the magazine was already inside, clustered by the home team's bench.

She walked over quickly, blowing on her fingers as she went. As requested, the management had lifted the basketball flooring, leaving the rink bare. With only a handful of people in the cavernous space, the building was cold. Figured. It seemed that Claire had felt cold for the last five years or so.

She rubbed her hands together and approached the group. Trish was busy talking on her cell phone. Her assistant, Elaine, also clad in fur and leather—though how she could afford it on an assistant's pitiful salary was beyond Claire—was talking to a heavy-set man in a blue suit. He, in turn, was carrying a large walkie-talkie. Must be the Garden's manager, Claire figured.

Meanwhile, a small gaggle of young males was huddled near or on the ice. One row up, on his own cell phone, was an intense-looking, well-groomed man in his thirties. Slicked-back hair. Black cashmere coat. The type of coat that owed its origins to well-groomed sheep and top negotiating skills. Claire would bet her newly purchased fifty-dollar tube of moisturizer that he was Jason Doyle's agent.

And within an easy, fifteen percent reach of that well-tailored arm was the man himself. Why else would a throng of men be acting with the giddiness of acne-riddled adolescents at a high school mixer? Claire heard snatches of conversation as she approached. Phrases such as "Stanley Cup play-offs," "number of assists" and "babes" punctuated the talk. Boys will be boys, no matter what age, she thought.

"Hey, guys, I hate to break up this little group, but business is business," Claire announced. One of the technical crew, a young fellow with an earring and the requisite straggly goatee, stepped out of the way, revealing a clear sighting of Jason Doyle, who was signing a few autographs. He looked up at the sound of her voice.

Unconsciously she tucked the gray lock of hair behind her ear. Her chin-length bob was chosen strictly for practicality. More often than not, she cut it herself; a habit that seemed to distress the hairdressers she visited intermittently. Their hand-waving bursts of enthusiasm about letting her thick, wavy hair frame her prominent cheekbones and accentuate her heart-shaped jaw, and their coloratura songs of praise for the wonders of highlights, didn't seem to justify the many hours required to spend sitting in a hairdresser's chair, draped in a plastic cape that invariably made Claire sweat in places she didn't know she had glands.

"Sorry to interrupt, but could you just show me where you've stowed the gear?" Claire asked. "I also need to talk to someone about the lighting. If we're shooting this in color, I'd like to have more light."

"Righto." The lanky techie bounded off, taking huge steps, to speak with Mr. Walkie-Talkie.

"I'm impressed."

Claire didn't need to look over to know who was talking. Even without raising his voice, Jason Doyle's delivery had enough firepower to knock a tin can off a fence railing from twenty feet away. She turned her head and felt caught in the crosshairs of his stare. "It's my naturally authoritative air," she said, no longer feeling quite so confident.

"It certainly made me snap to attention. Siegfrid and Roy could learn a thing or two from you." Jason walked toward her, the hangers-on peeling away reluctantly.

"Well, I usually draw the line at large animals with claws."

"You sure about that?" He held out his hand. Claire noticed that his nails were clipped short, but the sinews on the back of his large hands attested to a sizable strength. "I didn't realize outside that you must be—"

"Claire Marsden." Someone else's well-manicured hand reached Claire's first. "I'm Vernon Ehrenreich, Jason's agent. It's a pleasure to meet you. Though I must confess, I'm a little surprised to see you're the photographer for the story. I thought you were more a newsperson."

Claire gave Vernon a pinched smile and was just about to give him something else when Trish rapidly descended on them, a remarkable accomplishment considering her spike heels.

"Vernon, Claire, I see you've already made the introductions." Trish snapped shut her cell phone. "I can't tell you how lucky we are to have Claire. Didn't I tell you we wanted to capture a journalistic flair for the art? After all, what better way to portray a man of motion like Jason? In fact, when I mentioned Claire's name to Jason, he jumped at the opportunity."

That last bit of information was news to Claire. And for all she knew, it was also news to Jason Doyle, but he didn't appear to question the statement. Claire shifted her weight from one foot to the other and waited. Trish could talk a vacuum cleaner salesman into buying brooms. Not that she felt she needed to be defensive. Claire was proud of her credentials. True, sports had never been her beat, and she was not a celebrity photographer by any stretch of the imagination. But the Claire Marsden photo credit carried a lot of weight in the publishing world. And Trish had assured her up and down, left, right and center, that her background would not be an issue.

So here was Vernon, clearly angling to protect the bankable quality of his star.

"Action is one thing. But I thought we were talking sports photographer. No offense, Claire." Vernon held up a deferential hand. Claire nodded coolly. What she wouldn't give for a stray pigeon to suddenly drop a not so little gift on Vernon's gelled head. No, maybe on his coat. The sight of blemished cashmere might send him into anaphylactic shock.

"I supposed a Pulitzer counts for nothing?" Trish interjected.

Jason turned to Claire. "A Pulitzer?"

Claire shrugged. "Actually, it's two."

"Well, you may not value Claire's news experience, but I'm sure you saw January's *Focus Magazine* with Clyde Allthorpe on the cover?" Trish went on.

Claire saw Vernon's jaw drop. Who hadn't seen the magazine cover showing the running back, dripping with water, with a giddy grin adorning his face and, what appeared to be, little else on the rest of his body? The issue had set a record for the most newsstand copies ever sold. It had made every television entertainment show, and even become the running joke of late-night television hosts. Public radio had wanted to do an analysis of the phenomenon. What more could a girl ask for in the way of fame and fortune?

Well, she could have the fame and fortune of Clyde Allthorpe, who, as Vernon knew only too well, was the proud possessor of the largest endorsement contract among professional athletes. It was even an endorsement contract that eclipsed Jason's, which as timing would have it, was due for renegotiation. And speaking of renegotiation, Clyde had signed that contract *after* the cover photo had hit the stands.

"You took that photo?" Vernon asked Claire.

"I did," Claire said. "But you've got to understand—"

"What's to understand?" Trish interrupted. "I think Vernon fully appreciates how lucky we are to have you on this job. Now why don't you and Jason get to work while I talk to Vernon about what we're planning next." Trish shooed Claire and Jason along as if they were naughty puppies. There were times when well-manicured French tips definitely made a statement.

Claire turned to Jason. "Well, I guess we've got our marching orders. As you've already heard, I'm Claire Marsden, but I never got a chance to properly introduce myself." She held out her hand.

Jason took it. "You're freezing." He placed both her bare hands in his and started to rub. His hands were large, his skin rough. Claire didn't know about her hands, but her toes, which usually were frozen nubs despite two layers of woolen socks, were definitely getting hot. "You should wear gloves," he said, and rubbed more briskly.

Claire swallowed. "Can't. It's an occupational hazard. I can't wear gloves with the camera. I'm just always cold."

Jason lifted her hands in his and started to blow. "Better?"

Actually, she was feeling warm, quite warm. "I'm not sure better is the exact word I'd choose."

Jason peered over their hands. "Am I making you uncomfortable?" He didn't look the least bit concerned.

"How about maybe you stop?"

"How about maybe you blow on my hands and I'll see how *I* feel?"

Claire was just about to tell Jason what he could do to his hands when he released hers. He held up his hands in surrender. "Just kidding."

"Something tells me you're going to be bad news, Jason Doyle." She shook her head and searched for the technician who was to bring her cameras. He was over by the entrance to the ice rink. Bags of equipment were piled on a bench nearby. She motioned for Jason to follow.

"So how do you want me?" he asked.

Claire made a show of rummaging through her camera bag.

"Does this mean we're not going to be close friends?"

She looked up. "I think this photo session will be perfectly cordial. We'll relax, have fun. Afterward, we'll probably exchange Christmas cards for a year or two. I'll send you a congratulatory e-mail regarding your next Stanley Cup victory. You might send me pictures when your first child is born. But after that, even the most casual communication will peter out, and five years from now, you'll think, 'I wonder what ever happened to that lady photographer, Claire something? I remember she was good at her job, but, boy, was she ever lousy at taking a joke.'"

He listened in silence, and when she'd finished, took a step closer. His hulking frame was mere inches from hers. The worn leather of his jacket sleeve brushed against her sweater as he circled to get in her view. "Is it just me, or are you always this uptight, Claire Marsden?"

She turned, her face now mere inches from his. The color of his eyes had deepened to a midnight hue. Not good. She chickened out. Lowered her gaze. And saw his chest heave in a slow, hypnotic rhythm. Even the molecules of air that barely separated their bodies seemed to twitch and tremble in a sharp staccato.

She fixed what she hoped was an aloof gaze back on him, and, working hard to keep her voice calm, said, "Why don't you put on your skates and team jersey? We'll get you on the ice, doing your thing." The soul of business, she turned back to her camera bag and searched around for rolls of film. She stuffed them into the pockets of her jeans, and swung the camera strap over her neck with an ease borne of having repeated the motion at least a million times.

"Where do you want my hands?"

Claire nearly dropped her telephoto lens. So much for instinct.

"What do you want me to do with my hands—on the ice?" Jason had doffed his jacket and pulled on a jersey. He was sitting on the bench, lacing up his skates, something he, too, had done more than a million times.

The act should have been merely mechanical. Why was the sight of his strong fingers working with deft speed so sexy? Until she looked down at her own hands, Claire hadn't realized that she was unconsciously outlining the protruding camera lens. She quickly let go. The weight made the strap bite into the back of her neck

Claire straightened her shoulders and cleared her throat. "Well, I think we'll have you holding a stick and taking a few shots at the net." She wet her lips. "I understand that's what you're good at."

Jason finished lacing up. "Wait till you see me in action, Claire Marsden."

"Oh, I think I already have."

SHE WAS WRONG. In action—in motion—Jason Doyle was beyond great. Barely harnessed power positively radiated from his being. Dynamite was too passive an adjective. It was like being on the surface of the sun with those vortices of energy swirling in every direction.

Which only irritated Claire more because she was convinced she wasn't capturing it all on film. For a good forty-five minutes, she directed the crew while he swiftly skated up and down. He took slap shot after slap shot, pausing only when the lights needed repositioning—a process that was annoyingly time-consuming to Claire. She was used to capturing the photo as quickly as possible. But the professional and perfectionist in her knew that the technical adjustments were key to getting these color shots right.

"Would you move them to either side of the goal? That's it, a little higher on the stands. And, Jason, take the shots right on goal, okay?" She moved behind the net.

"Don't trust me enough to stand in front? I hardly ever miss a stationary target, you know?" He leaned on his stick.

"I'm not concerned for me, but my camera. Any loss of concentration might do it in."

"Always the ready excuse to keep from getting close." He lined up a row of pucks.

"Gosh, I don't know why the thought of having a speeding puck fly within millimeters of my face just doesn't do it for me." Claire held up her camera and crouched behind the net.

"Must be a testosterone thing."

"If the shoe fits."

"Among other things."

Claire lowered her camera, but before she even finished uttering, "Hey," he stepped up to the first puck and with machinelike precision sent each one in the line hurtling toward her face.

She quickly raised her camera and focused. Natural instinct had her flinching the first time the shot came flying toward her, only the loose mesh protecting the bones of her face. It was like being in front of a firing squad. She held firm and let the shutter whir, determined to get her shots of his shots.

Ten minutes later, soaked with as much sweat as he was, Claire wasn't convinced. She chewed on her lower lip. She wanted the reader to not just see the power, but to actually feel it. She shook her head and rewound, opening the camera and flipping the roll into her bag.

Jason skated up, spraying ice chips as he came to a screeching halt next to her. He was breathing hard. The cold air made his breath cloud. Claire looked up. She quickly popped in a new roll of film. "That's it! Keep doing that. And get more light in here. Now. Fast. And keep doing that heavy breathing."

"That's what all the women say."

Claire didn't bother to look up from her viewfinder. "I just bet they do." She rattled off the shots until the air cleared. "We've got to get you moving again." She snapped her fingers. "But hold on a sec." She looked for the same lanky techie who had helped her out earlier. "Why don't you rustle up a pair of skates for me? Size eight."

Jason stopped making lazy eights with his stick. "You skate?"

"It's been a while, but I think I'll be good enough." Claire looked around the rink. The last time she was on skates was when she was a teenager. She'd been in Holland with Big Jim. They'd just come back from Thailand, and as Big Jim exclaimed—Big Jim never just said anything; he always had to announce it to the world—"It's colder than a witch's tit." In Big Jim's mind that meant it was prime time for drinking and outdoor sports. The exact order of which tended to get a little fuzzy. "We're here in Hans Brinker country, Claire-y," she remembered him proclaiming. "We've got to skate on the canals."

And skate they did, along with scores of Dutch parents and their laughing children. The hours on the frozen ice were followed by hours in a pub, with Big Jim putting away endless bottles of beer and regaling the clientele with a bottomless well of tales.

"You sure you're up to it?" Jason's voice penetrated her memories.

Claire looked over. "No problem. Look, here comes Elaine." She nodded toward Trish's assistant and slid across the rink. At the bench, she quickly laced up. Her feet felt uncomfortable as she wiggled her ankles. "Well, here goes nothing."

Claire's first steps on the ice were tentative. Then she relaxed her knees and quickly built up a rhythm of pushing off and gliding, an easy rocking from one skate to the other. She circled in a wide arc near the entrance to the rink, picked up speed and skated back to the center of the ice where Jason stood in the face-off circle.

Jason watched her as she approached. "Not bad."

"I'm no Sonja Henje, let alone Wayne Gretzky, but it'll

do." She picked up her camera in both hands. "Listen, ditch the jersey."

Jason held the uniform top by the V-neck. "This?"

"That's right." Claire made a throwing motion with her hand.

"You're the boss." Jason slipped it over his head, leaving only the tight black T-shirt—and very little else—to the imagination.

An "ohmygod!" was audible from where Trish was standing by the boards. Then a clump. Claire looked over and saw her bending to retrieve her cell phone.

"Just think what could happen if I went further?" Jason dipped a hand under the bottom edge of his T-shirt and started to lift.

Claire caught a glimpse of his granite-smooth stomach muscles. She swallowed with difficulty. "No, I think you've gone far enough. I wouldn't want Trish to end up face forward."

"I'm fully qualified at CPR. Trish would be in good hands."

And she was sure that Trish would be only too willing to take a dive to test out his claim. Which, come to think of it, was just what she had in mind originally. So why did she find herself wanting to see Jason practice his life-resuscitating skills on her, instead of her best friend? Down, girl, down, she admonished.

"Hold that thought. You can play doctor later," she said. "Guys—" she motioned to the crew "—spread the lights up and down the rink, away from the boards. And, Jason, I want you to skate straight down the ice, not too fast. I'll skate along with you. I want you to be handling the puck. Look ahead, like you're planning a shot on goal."

He took off slowly. "Like this?"

"You can go a little faster. Good. That's it. Keep looking ahead. You can talk if you want."

He handled the puck deftly. "So how come you didn't ask me to take off my shirt, but you gave Clyde Allthorpe the go-ahead?"

"I didn't have to ask."

Jason stopped abruptly, the edges of his blades leaving a layer of white powder. "He was already au naturel?"

Claire kept her eye in the viewfinder. "Don't stop. Keep going. And no, he was not au naturel, as you put it. He was swimming with his fiancée, Donna. And he was wearing swimming trunks—little tiny ones. Bright blue. Very cute."

"I can imagine." Jason didn't sound all that pleased.

"No, don't look at me. Straight ahead. That's it. Great. Anyway, like I said, they were just getting out of the pool when I took the photo. They'd been swimming together, very happy. Over the top, actually. Their wedding was the next day. In fact, I was there to shoot their wedding."

"You were on assignment?"

"Not exactly. I'd met Clyde when he was on an aid mission to Ethiopia. We hit it off, and he asked me if I'd shoot his wedding. It was all very hush-hush, no announcements. When the press got a whiff of it, Clyde and Donna decided the best thing would be to make arrangements to release photos to just one magazine. I talked it over with them, contacted Trish, and of course she jumped at the idea." She stopped to reload, and Jason pulled up next to her.

"I bet she did." Jason looked over at Trish, who was chatting up Vernon but still managed to keep a cell phone plastered to one ear. Her blond hair sparkled in the glare of the lights, giving her sophisticated beauty an ethereal glow. It was Tinker Bell with sex appeal.

"So what's this about Trish needing a husband? I would think she'd be able to pick and choose. Wait a minute—she doesn't need a husband because she is in the family way, so to speak? I'm not risking a paternity suit."

"No, she is not in the family way, so to speak, and don't look so panic-stricken. Besides, I didn't say she needed a husband. I said she needed a fiancé." Claire pursed her lips. "Listen, let's skate down the middle of the ice toward the net at the other end. I want to get a shot of you head-on." She started to skate backward, looking through the camera. "That's it. Skate toward me. No, don't look at me. Look over my shoulder, like you're scoping out the defense. That's it. That's great."

Jason timed his longer strides to her shorter ones. "So why does she need a fiancé?"

"She doesn't need a fiancé exactly, more like a pretend fiancé. You see it's like this—we have to go to this wedding of a former boyfriend of hers, and she doesn't want him to know she's unattached. It's a pride thing." She kept clicking the shutter. "That's it. Breathe a little harder through your mouth."

"Ah, the heavy-breathing thing again." He puffed out dramatically. "And this ex-boyfriend is supposed to believe that Trish and I are passionately in love?"

"We'll say you two met on this story and suddenly felt this overwhelming attraction. I mean, look at the two of you. Beauty and brawn."

"I presume I'm the beauty."

Claire rolled her eyes. "Glamorous careers. Jet-setting lifestyles. It's perfect."

"So do you need a fiancé, too?"

Claire kept her head behind the camera. "Nope. No problems with prior attachments."

"Any plans for the future?"

"No, I'm a free agent, and I'm happy just the way I am."

"But you'll be there? At the wedding, I mean?"

"Of course. Who do you think the wedding photographer is?"

"I should have known. Have camera will travel. You know, I gotta warn you." He sped up his skating.

"Not too close. I can't focus that close with this lens." It wasn't just the lens that was having trouble, as his body space impinged on hers.

"I have to tell you something."

"Tell me what?" Her back bumped into the crossbar of the net with a jolt. She would have dropped her camera if the strap hadn't been around her neck.

"I tried to tell you." Jason put his hand on her back and massaged the point where she had banged into the bar.

Claire tried not to think about the further pain he was causing.

"I'm beginning to think you need me more than you realize." He slowly rubbed her shoulder blades.

Claire's head shot up. "Just because I banged into the net doesn't mean I need you. And you can stop rubbing now. I didn't do that much damage."

"Ah, you don't know how much damage you've already done. In any case, there's something else I need to tell you."

"Something else?" She felt a strange letdown when Jason removed his hand.

"Yes, not only do you ride a motorcycle, you also skate backward. As it turns out, these are two of my requirements for a wife. And I must say, you pass with flying colors."

"You're joking, right?"

Jason grinned over his shoulder and started to glide away. "Oh, by the way. My keys?"

Claire swore under her breath. She fished into her jeans' pocket and tossed them underhand. He caught them with an easy swipe and skated away, only to stop and return in a long slow arc.

"Yes?" She scowled as he slid in close. Again, too close. He lifted one hand.

She watched his hand come close to her face. Then closer. "You want to tell me what's going on here?"

With a gentle swipe of his index finger, Jason brushed the corner of her mouth. She flinched. Felt her lips tingle and her tongue turn dry. Gulping was impossible. Inhaling only slightly more doable. He had to know how awkward she was feeling.

Jason smiled broadly. He knew. "Powdered sugar."

Claire's eyes widened. "Powdered sugar?"

Jason brought his index finger to his mouth and slowly tasted it. "Yup, definitely powdered sugar. Must have been that donut you were eating when I first rolled up." He looked down, one eyebrow slightly cocked.

The photographer in Claire leapt to take the pose.

The woman in her was paralyzed.

"And by the way, Claire Marsden," Jason said lazily over his shoulder as he skated off for a second time. "That was no joke."

Claire slowly brought her hand to her face and touched the corner of her open mouth. Her skin was hot, incredibly hot. She couldn't possibly be blushing. She never blushed. But then she'd never been touched by a demon on skates, either.

3

CLAIRE PACED in front of Trish. "You let me go through that whole shoot with powdered sugar on my face!"

"You told him I needed a fiancé?" Trish responded. She darted her head around to see if they were being overheard. She had all the subtlety of a silent film star. The closest person was Elaine. She was over by the bench, talking with the straggly bearded techie. He somehow didn't seem her type. "Jason probably thinks I'm pathetic."

"Trust me. He doesn't think you're pathetic." Claire remembered the appreciative look Jason had shown Trish as they got off the ice. Trish, who was looking so together, so sleek. While she, Claire, had a drippy nose and freezing, cramped toes. Sniffling and hobbling—she sounded like two of the Seven Dwarfs. And that's when she remembered she still had on the skates.

She sat and began yanking them off. "I don't know why you think anyone would think you're pathetic. You weren't the one tripping over her own two feet on the ice, all the while having this white glob on your face. Why didn't you tell me?" Claire yanked off the second skate and looked around for her boots.

Trish crossed her arms. "Why so touchy about a little bit of sugar on your face? Frankly, I didn't even notice."

Claire found one work boot and pulled it on. She didn't bother to lace it up. "That's because your eyes were elsewhere." Claire got on her hands and knees and started scouting under the bench for her other boot.

"He is rather attractive, isn't he? One could do far worse in the fiancé category. In fact, it might be something worth contemplating seriously—in a very preliminary stage, of course."

Claire heard the flirtatious lilt to Trish's voice as she scrounged around on the rubber flooring for her lost boot. Her hand touched something sticky. She didn't want to think about the possibilities.

"So what did he say?"

"About what?" In the dank, dark recesses under the first row of permanent seating, Claire located her boot. It was pushed against the cement riser.

"You know, about pretending to be my fiancé at the wedding?" Trish must have bent down because her voice was louder.

Claire shimmied out backward, deciding the safest route out was the same way she'd come in. She dragged the boot behind her. "We never got that far. Why don't you ask him yourself?" Her derriere emerged from the deep abyss.

"Ask me what?"

Claire banged the back of her head on the bottom of a metal seat. She dropped her boot and it tumbled into the great netherworld of discarded chewing gum and Raisinets. No doubt Jason was looking down at her rear end as she hesitated on all fours. She could crawl back under. But then there was that mysterious sticky goo.

"You need a hand?" Jason's voice was louder, nearer. Much nearer.

In the shadowy darkness under the seats, Claire sensed immediately that he had joined her. She felt the ripples of energy that emanated from his body. If only he'd thought to bring a flashlight. "No need to bother. I'm fine, thank you."

"The lady doth protest too much."

"And the jock knows a literary line or two. I'm impressed. But truly, I wouldn't advise scrounging around here unless you've had a recent tetanus shot. Besides, I'm just looking for my boot. I had it a minute ago and I seem to have lost it again." Claire groped with her hand. She landed on something. It definitely wasn't sticky. And it definitely wasn't her boot.

It was large. It was strong. Sinews ridged the skin. Knuckles defined the contours. Fingers slightly curled; nails blunt cut. And there wasn't the hint of a wedding ring. It was power at rest. But it hardly made Claire feel restful.

"Whoops, sorry about that." Claire turned her head.

"Don't be. It could happen to anyone." In the darkness he moved his head toward hers. He shifted his hand.

His movement caused Claire to realize that her hand was still on his. "Oh, sorry." She started to pull it away, but he switched grips, holding her fingers lightly.

The sudden dizziness enveloping her head had to be due to the awkward position she was in, Claire told herself. She cleared her throat, if not her brain functions. "I think my boot may be over by your hand."

She leaned awkwardly in that direction. And felt her mouth brush his cheek.

Jason turned. His lips accidentally touched hers.

His lips pressed lightly. Maybe not an accident? It was brief. Lips ever so slightly parted. Warm breaths and tumbling heartbeats mixing.

And it was the most mind-numbing experience of Claire's life. And it was happening under the seat of a hockey rink.

"You guys all right down there?"

Trish's voice penetrated the haze of emotions that engulfed Claire. She felt Jason's hand tighten briefly before he let go.

"No problem. We were just searching for Claire's boot. I think I found it." He searched with his other hand, passing it to Claire.

She was surprised she could still mumble thanks. Backing out on her hands and knees, she slowly rose.

"Find something interesting down there?" Trish rested one hand on her hip.

Claire shivered. "You don't want to know." She dropped her boot to the ground and worked it on with her toes. Jason got to his feet, as well. He raked his hand through his thick hair.

"Well, come now," Trish announced. "Enough of this hide-and-seek. Vernon has agreed to leave you in our care, Jason, for the rest of today's schedule." She flounced her coat more squarely on her shoulders. "Why don't you leave that motorbike of yours here while we take a taxi uptown to the hospital?" Trish waved in the general direction of Elaine, who looked as if she was starting to lose interest in her Mr. Right. "Elaine can drive it up and meet us there."

"Claire maybe, Elaine never," Jason said.

"I'm only too happy." Claire walked over and grabbed her camera bag. Whatever distance she could put between herself and Jason would be a welcome blessing.

"Don't be ridiculous, Claire. We need you close by. We can always send a security guard. What's more to the point—" Trish grabbed Jason's arm "—when we're all alone in the taxi, I want to know what you think about the fiancé thing." Claire trailed behind as Trish kept her half nelson grip on Jason. "I realize it's an imposition, and it was highly unprofessional of Claire to mention it to you during a session."

"Maybe I will ride the bike after all," Claire murmured.

"What's that, Claire?" Trish stuck out her hand for a cab. The ones that sped by had their lights on, indicating they were occupied. "I should have had Elaine arrange for a car service to pick us up." She dug in her Prada shoulder bag and pulled out her cell phone. "I can still have her do it."

Claire saw some commuters eyeing Jason. It was only a matter of time before they were surrounded. "Never mind about Elaine." She spotted a taxi barreling down the other side of Sixth Avenue, stepped off the curb, and with her thumb and middle finger forming a circle, delivered a piercing whistle.

Like Odysseus responding to the sirens's call, the cab made a suicidal move through the traffic and shrieked to a halt. All that was lacking was for it to be dashed against the rocks. Luckily, the curbs in Manhattan are low and rounded.

Trish snapped her cell phone shut. "I'd forgotten that little trick of yours." She let Jason hold open the car door, then got into the back seat first.

Jason waited for Claire to get in next. "You realize you just demonstrated requirement number three." He pantomimed her whistling.

Claire stared at the way his fingers touched his open mouth. And found her libido bouncing around with all the manic exuberance of a two-month-old Labrador retriever. "Boy, you're easy to please. Half the women in the world must meet your requirements. And if you don't get in the taxi soon, a few of them will be joining us any minute."

They bundled in, Claire in the middle. Her camera bag rested on her lap. Jason didn't seem much farther away. "You can't move a little?" She looked down at his thigh pressed up against her leg.

Jason leaned over to speak to Trish, ignoring Claire's comment. "So, tell me about the wedding." His jacket sleeve put pressure on Claire's shoulder.

Claire pursed her lips and studied the taxi driver's license displayed on the dashboard.

"It's really very simple. Claire, David and I all went to high school together in Leeds Springs," Trish explained quickly.

"Leeds Springs?" Jason asked.

"A suburban town north of New York City."

"Think country clubs and golf courses," Claire said. She focused on the driver's name, trying to decide which eastern European country he had come from. One with an overabundance of "k's" it seemed.

Jason turned to Claire. "You lived in suburbia?"

She shrugged. "Only a year and a half. I survived. So did it."

"Yes, well, all three of us were inseparable, mainly because we all worked on the school newspaper. Claire was the photographer, David covered sports, and I, well, not to be immodest, but I was the editor-in-chief."

"Why am I not surprised?" Jason said. Claire decided to kick him for that smug little comment.

"Anyway, to make a long story short, David was my first true love, something that's very special to a woman," Trish went on.

Claire eyed Jason. "Don't even go there," she warned sotto voce. He placed his hand on his chest. Who me? he seemed to indicate. She kicked him again.

Jason winced. "Has anyone ever told you that you have violent instincts?"

She stared wide-eyed. Only a newborn calf could have looked more innocent. "Sorry, my foot slipped."

"Twice?"

"Repetitive stress syndrome?"

"And even though we all went our separate ways, we stayed in touch." Trish cupped her chin wistfully. "Call me unrealistic, but somehow I thought one day he'd come back into my life. Only I never envisioned we'd meet again at a wedding—his wedding, to someone else. To an orthodontist no less." Trish took a pair of sunglasses from her bag and wrestled them onto her face. "An orthodontist," she harrumphed.

"I'm sure she has very nice teeth," Claire said.

"Don't try to be nice, Claire. It doesn't suit you." Trish fiddled with the bow of her glasses, designer ones, naturally. "Anyway, even though David's moved to Chicago—he's a district attorney—" she turned to Jason "—they've decided to get married back at his parents' place in Westchester, a nice Tudor place right by the golf course. I always did think it would make the perfect place for a wedding."

Trish paused, as if visualizing the outdoor seating arrangement of her dreams—lilacs and lilies of the valley roped in garlands along white satin-covered folding chairs, a veritable aromatherapy of connubial bliss. "Well, when the invitation came, I accepted as a matter of course, and replied I would be bringing a guest. The thing of it is, to make this really work—to attend from a real position of strength—what I need is not just a guest, but a fiancé. That way I truly look like..." For once in her life, Trish actually needed to pause.

"Like you're sleeping with someone?" Claire offered.

"That you have someone who is special, a lover," Jason corrected.

Trish turned and pulled off her glasses. "Claire, you're so predictable. But, Jason, you're really quite sensitive, aren't you?"

Claire rolled her eyes. "Sensitive is not the adjective I would have chosen."

"But then words are not your line of work, are they?" Jason shifted his weight and put his arm over the back of the seat. His hand casually rested on Claire's shoulder. She hunched forward and hugged her bag.

"And what makes it even more incredible, Jason, is you're clearly amazingly handsome and famous," Trish said.

Jason nudged Claire. "See, someone recognizes my better qualities." She hunched farther forward.

"But I'm not sure people are going to believe we're an item." From the emotional high of a second ago, Trish dipped to the depths of the Marianas Trench. "I mean the wedding's this Saturday. And we've only just met. Besides, it's not as if we have anything in common. I mean, I wouldn't know a hockey bat from a baseball bat."

Claire rolled her eyes. "It's a stick, Trish, a hockey stick." She would have said something further along those lines, but she saw that her friend truly looked despondent, only reinforcing Claire's long-standing belief that it never paid to fall in love. "Listen, sweetie, don't worry about the sports stuff. Didn't you ever hear of the theory that opposites attract? You can just say you met over this story, which is perfectly true. And there was this instantaneous spark. This spontaneous combustion."

Trish sniffed. "Spontaneous combustion?"

"This violent, passionate bolt of desire, which struck like lightning."

"Oh, that spontaneous combustion." Trish waved her hand dismissively and replaced her sunglasses. "Don't be ridiculous. That kind of thing never happens. I'm surprised that a cynic like you, Claire, would even mention something as silly as that. People just don't suddenly get all weak in the knees by some sudden onslaught of passion."

Claire stared at Jason. She saw him work his jaw. She immediately thought of their fleeting kiss. Her stomach contracted violently. "I suppose you're right," she said softly, still looking at his lips.

"Still, people will believe anything, won't they?" Trish sounded as if she was trying to convince herself. "And seeing as we could say it was this sudden thing, we could also say afterward that it broke up just as quickly—one of those sputtering flame things. So, will you do it?" She turned and rested a hand on Jason's sleeve.

Jason looked at Claire's lips.

"Jason?" Trish asked.

"Hmm?"

"Will you do it? Will you be my fiancé?"

He stared at Claire's mouth as he spoke. "There's still six weeks to the start of the season. And when you put it that way, how can I refuse."

THREE HOURS LATER, ensconced in the children's ward of an Upper East Side hospital and research institute, Claire had just about run out of film.

That wasn't the only thing to run out of steam. After going through several tapes and lobbing out questions that seemed to touch on everything from his first-grade teacher—Mrs. Greenberg, she wore a hairnet and orthopedic shoes—to the latest rumors about his hot-and-heavy affair with a Swedish cover girl—"We're just good friends," Claire heard him say over the whir of her camera—Trish packed up her recorder, her cell phone and her handheld organizer, and had Elaine arrange for a car to take her back to the office.

Someone else had yet to wilt, though. Jason was enthusiastically chatting away and signing autographs in the children's clinic. Despite the ever-present barrage of tubes and drips, the mood was pure upbeat, with Jason trading high-fives with most of the kids.

Claire circled a hospital bed as Jason joked with one boy about the cap he was wearing. "Hey," he called over to Claire, "don't take his picture unless he promises to get rid of that Rangers cap. It's Blades or nothing around here." Jason dug into a bag and pulled out a cap. "Now that's more like it."

The smiling boy, his head billiard-ball smooth, laughed as he doffed the Blades souvenir. "Hey, Jason, you fall for my trick every time. I must have four Blades caps from you already." The youngster adjusted the bill just right.

Jason held up a warning finger. "And that's going to be the last. At least for today." He pulled down the bill as Claire snapped another picture. "I'm all out of caps. Did everybody get one, Larry?" He looked to the doctor who was accompanying them.

"I think you've hit everyone, at least once, Jason." As the rest of the medical team, Larry—Dr. Lawrence Shepherd, head of pediatric oncology—wore bright colors instead of the usual white uniform. He had a silly-looking frog hanging off his stethoscope. It seemed to suit the middle-aged physician with the gimlet smile. "We'll see you back here in two weeks anyway, right?"

Jason nodded. "Got enough for the scrapbook,

Claire?" He got up off the bed, looking bone-weary but deep-down satisfied.

"You're a fraud, Jason Doyle," Claire said as she packed up. "Vernon churns out the usual publicity drivel about the swinging star-athlete making the requisite charity appearances, and here it actually looks like you enjoy it. Next you'll tell me you've been coming here off-the-record for five years."

"I'd say it's more like fifteen," Larry said as he walked them to the elevators. He pushed up his horn-rimmed glasses and looked at Jason.

"It's the food. I just can't get enough of it."

"Just bring the Stanley Cup to New York this coming season," Larry said. "I've got a twenty-dollar bet riding on it with the president of the hospital board."

"And here I thought I was appreciated for just being me." They walked companionably to the elevators, with Jason inquiring about how Larry's children had liked sleep-away camp. Without too much prompting, Larry opened his wallet.

"That's some catch." Claire leaned over to take a look at the snapshot. A boy of around ten with board shorts and a baseball cap turned backward was proudly holding a fish. A fishing pole stood at attention in the other hand.

"Largemouth bass. Must have been two pounds." Larry grinned before carefully packing up his wallet.

"Paging Dr. Shepherd. Dr. Lawrence Shepherd."

Larry looked up. "Never a dull moment." He held open the elevator, letting Claire and Jason enter without him. "Remember what I said." He looked at Jason.

"I know, the twenty dollars."

"That, and my usual invitation. It's always good any time you want."

The doors closed. Jason leaned back against the wall and closed his eyes. She let the day's first moment of silence embrace them before finally asking, "How come you know Larry? You're not from the city, right?"

"Nope, I'm one of St. Johnsbury, Vermont's finest. Larry was my college roommate's doctor. I never forgot what he did for Danny. Larry has a gift."

"I wouldn't say you're completely untalented. How many people can play hockey the way you do?"

Jason opened his eyes. "Did a goal ever save anyone's life?" He paused. "But enough humility on my part. Instead, let's turn to a far more intriguing subject—Claire Marsden." Whatever weariness or bitterness he may have felt was quickly masked.

"Trust me, it's just your run-of-the-mill, globe-trotting photojournalist stuff. Not a very interesting topic."

"Oh, I don't know. Let's start with this." Jason playfully tugged Claire's streak of gray hair. "I've been dying to know. It's real, yeah?"

"It's real, yeah. Do you know many thirty-year-old women who purposely put gray in their hair?"

Jason toyed with the dramatic lock. "I like it. It's different. It's you."

"Actually, it's more my father. He had the same streak. Turned gray around seventeen, eighteen, just like me. And that's what I inherited—besides seven hundred and forty-five dollars, a Leica in impeccable working order, and a good set of camera lenses."

"I'd say from your talent, you inherited a whole lot more." He toyed with her hair a bit longer. "And what did you inherit from your mother?"

Claire rescued her hair from his fingering and tucked it behind her ear. "If you met my mother, you wouldn't even bother to ask the question. Let's just say we're the yin and yang of mother-daughter relationships." The elevator doors opened at the hospital lobby. "Our eighteen months of living together were as baffling to her as they were to me. To her great consternation, I just never learned essential life lessons, like how to coordinate my handbag with my shoes."

Jason studied her work boots and canvas camera bag that doubled as a catch-all purse. "I noticed. It's one of your more charming qualities. I hadn't thought of it before, but I may add that to my requirements for a future wife. Let's see, where does that put you? Four in total?"

Claire swung open the wide glass door and walked outside. She waited under the canopy on the sidewalk. She looked around as he joined her. "I don't know what you're trying to accomplish with all this future wife rigmarole, but it's starting to get a little stale."

Jason zipped up his jacket. "Rigmarole. I like that. Whoever said words weren't your strength?"

Claire spun around. The man could try the patience of Mother Teresa. "All right, I'm just going to ignore whatever's going on."

"But why?"

"Well, for one thing, do I need to remind you that you're supposed to have fallen madly in love with Trish and are engaged to her?"

"That's pretend."

"Nevertheless." Claire pulled out the schedule from her back pocket and unfolded it. "Let's see. Tomorrow appears to be a full day. Eight o'clock tomorrow morning we hit your gym." She folded the paper back up. "A little workout's in store."

Jason wetted his lips, letting the tip of his tongue rest in the corner of his mouth. Never had a gesture of thoughtfulness been so X-rated.

"Hey, Jason, I don't know which gets more stares—you, or that damn bike of yours." The hospital doorman tossed him the keys. Jason's motorcycle had mysteriously rematerialized in front of the hospital.

"Thanks, Nick," he replied, then turned to Claire. "Can I give you a lift? I need both hands to steer, you know."

"Even without your hands, you're not to be trusted. I think I'll take my chances on the street." She took a few backward steps.

"Tomorrow." Jason nodded. "I'll be ready, Claire Marsden. Oh, which reminds me. Before, when you were explaining why you were going to ignore me, you said 'for one thing.' What I want to know is, what's the other reason?"

4

CLAIRE WAS READY.

But Trish wasn't. Neither was Elaine. Maybe they couldn't deal with putting on eyeliner and lipstick before sunrise two days in a row.

A certain member of the male population didn't seem to have those worries. Jason was there waiting, tapping his foot as he leaned against the check-in area in the Plaza's lobby. A giant arrangement of Asiatic lilies and birds-of-paradise, which was perched on the marble counter, quivered in time to his strict tattoo.

And talk about the opposite of all dressed up with no-where to go. Under his leather bomber jacket, he wore a ratty sweatshirt and sweatpants. On his feet, an old pair of sneakers held together with duct tape. There wasn't a logo in sight.

It was a sponsor's nightmare. And from the looks of the female clerks on duty, every woman's fantasy.

How could a man who'd just rolled out of bed and into yesterday's laundry possibly generate that much raw sex appeal? Claire wondered. Thoughts of his just rolling out of bed lingered in her imagination. She set her jaw and marched forward. Simply do your job, she told herself. No weak knees today.

Jason spotted her instantly and pushed himself away from the desk with his elbows. Claire stopped two feet in front of him and performed an obvious once-over.

"Don't overdress on my account," she said in greeting him.

Jason leaned over and picked up a canvas backpack. "I figured I'd change into my formal wear for when we go house hunting."

"Always important to impress the co-op boards." After Jason's morning workout, Claire was supposed to capture his search for the perfect abode in his new hometown. She couldn't wait to see what marvel of mirrored glass and steel he would choose for himself. Her image of bachelor jocks living alone fit with some slick, Donald Trump skyscraper on the Upper East Side.

"Vernon not joining us?" She let the doorman hail a taxi out front.

"No, he has to hold some Romanian gymnast's hand today. I've been upstaged by an eighty-pound tumbler." He didn't look stricken. "What about Trish? Still too early for her nail polish to dry?"

"Don't be so hard on Trish." Claire defended her friend, even though there might be a grain of truth in Jason's crack. "She may get a little carried away at times—"

"Trust me. No man would ever complain about a woman getting carried away. At anytime."

Claire frowned and was about to snap back a retort when she caught herself. Jason had this unerring way of getting her goat. She had always considered herself fairly immune to "male speech." After years of living in close quarters with war correspondents and soldiers, she had developed a tough skin when it came to many things—constant innuendos being only one of them.

But conversations with Jason seemed to leave her as vulnerable as a schoolmarm. Why did he always seem to know which button to push? She must be getting soft in her old age. These days, after all, she was in the habit of sleeping on clean sheets—Pratese, Trish had informed her—and having a cleaning lady to do her wash—never had her T-shirts been so cuddly soft and April-fresh smelling.

That was it! It was all that fabric softener. It was affecting her brain as well as her nasal passages.

Satisfied that she had a petrochemical explanation for her softening response system, Claire squared her shoulders with a renewed sense of self-confidence and replied with her customary glibness. "I must remember that insight the next time the Secretary General of the United Nations asks me for my opinion on global warming. In the meantime, I'd like to discuss some of Patti's other admirable traits."

"Patti?" A taxi pulled up, and Jason gave the address.

"Sorry, Trish. Trish used to be known as Patti back in high school, but she decided to change it."

"Before or after sleeping with the sports editor?"

Claire turned to him in the back seat of the taxi. "As surprising as this may be to you, the change was not part of some post-coital response. 'Oh, now that I am a woman, I think I'll change my name to Trish.'"

Jason leaned back in his seat and gave her a wide-eyed stare. "That is hard to believe."

Claire stared back, taking in his look of mock amazement. "You're enjoying this, aren't you?"

He tilted his head. "Very much so. Aren't you?"

Claire smiled thoughtfully. "I guess I am, too." And she was. Despite her earlier misgivings, she found herself amused, maybe relaxed. No, not relaxed. "Anyway, to make a long explanation short—Trish used to be known as Patti because her name is really Patricia. But then she thought that sounded too Gidget-ish."

He leaned forward. "I realize that's supposed to make it all crystal-clear, but who or what is a Gidget?"

"Never mind. That's not important. What is important is that Trish took me under her wing when I first showed up in Leeds Springs. I had never lived in America, never heard of the suburban high school scene. I was so out, I didn't even know there was such a thing as an 'in' crowd. And Trish immediately made me part of the newspaper crowd, made me feel accepted. And her generosity didn't end there. Later, when I'd be between assignments and back in the States, she always let me crash at her place, even kept a trunk with all my stuff. I'm there now as a matter of fact."

"She seems like quite a friend."

"The best. It's on account of her that I'm shooting this job." She turned to face Jason. The taxi turned sharply at the corner.

"I'd say it was probably talent that got you the job. It's probably just as much to Trish's benefit, if not more, that you're shooting the pictures." He looked deadly serious.

Claire scoffed. "Come off it. We all know that in this world, talent only gets you so far. Well, maybe not in your world, but in mine, anyway. It's who you know that counts. If I can help out Trish, great. But bottom line, she's the one who hired me."

"Were you always this cynical?"

"You can call it cynical if you want. I prefer to think of it as realistic. In any case, it's important to me that Trish doesn't get hurt with this whole wedding business. Very important." Claire studied her hands. She realized she'd been folding and unfolding them on top of her camera case.

"Claire?" he asked softly. "Claire?" he asked again. She looked up. "I understand your loyalty, and I applaud it. Heck, you're talking to someone who plays on a team as a profession. But I want you to get one thing straight." He paused.

Relieved to see that the taxi had stopped, Claire leaned against the door, ready to get out.

Jason put a hand on her arm. His voice was low, barely above a whisper. "I will make sure that everything goes okay for Trish at the wedding. But get one thing clear, crystal-clear." He tightened his grip on her arm. Claire looked at the hand on her jacket sleeve, then at his face. There wasn't a grin in sight. And just when she would have preferred him to tease her in some good-natured, tasteless way, he said, in a deadly serious tone, "I'm not doing this because it's important to Trish. I'm doing it because it's important to you." And then he let go of her arm.

CLAIRE SWUNG open the door, climbed out, and adjusted the awkward load of her camera bag. She gulped for air, any air, to counter the sudden attack of hyperventilation that had seized her. And she was having a hard time blaming it on laundry products.

Jason Doyle is an assignment, she told herself firmly. And he's the means to helping out a good friend. Period. What she needed now in her life was the safety of simplicity. No complications. No risks. Just uninterrupted nights of sleep, regular meals and a paycheck every two weeks.

What she didn't need was Jason Doyle messing with her brain, and messing with the rest of her insides. And right now she was definitely having a mind-body experience, one that wasn't leading to a greater state of bliss. No amount of self-help gurus, green tea or lavender bath salts was going to provide an antidote, either. What she needed had to be far more potent—one-hundred-percent caffeine.

She turned back and watched as Jason paid the driver. He slung his backpack over his shoulder. His jacket rose to expose his hipbones, jutting against the low-slung, soft fabric of his sweatpants. She gulped and turned away quickly. "I desperately need coffee," she gasped. She was going to need it intravenously if his pants slipped any lower.

She looked around for a coffee shop, taking in her surroundings for the first time. "What are we doing in the Village?" So intent had she been during the conversation in the cab that she hadn't paid any attention to where they were going. "I thought we were going to the gym." She'd naturally assumed they were using a training facility at the Garden. Or if not, some posh health club, with state-of-the-art machines and freshly squeezed carrot and guava juice in a carefully constructed snack bar.

She turned a three-sixty on her heels. When she thought of the Village, she thought of jazz clubs, wacky Halloween parades, and shops selling rhinestone handcuffs and crotchless underpants. She didn't think of strapping specimens of male beauty—at least not in the context of professional sports. But here they were, on the edge of the New York University campus, not exactly a powerhouse in hockey.

"I would have thought you usually worked out with the team," she said again.

"That's true. They have special equipment tailored to building up quads and hamstrings for lateral movement."

Claire nodded, not having the faintest idea what he was talking about.

"But I also like to scout out universities. It's something

I got into the habit of doing when I was with my last team. Their gyms may not have the shiniest equipment, but the gym rats are really eager. Nothing pushes you harder than a bunch of cocky twenty-year-olds watching your every move."

Why anyone would voluntarily want to compete against guys who could party all night, live on bags of Oreos, and still come out and run a sub-five-minute mile, was beyond her comprehension. Unless you still felt you could do the same thing. She studied Jason. "I suppose you think you can drink shots of tequila all night and still outrun, out jump and out lift any of them."

"I can't?" Jason looked incredulous.

If he didn't look so boyishly handsome in his sloppy clothes and unkempt hair—no, there was nothing boyish about Jason Doyle—Claire would have clocked him right there and then. Talk about delusional. The man thought he was immortal, or at least immortally young. Chalk up another reason for her to steer clear. In her experience, people with an unnatural sense of their own invincibility tended to do reckless things that got themselves and others into trouble. Big trouble.

"Well, some of us are mature enough to realize that we need to take care of our bodies, to nourish them with essential vitamins. That being the case, I'm going over there to get coffee." She pointed to an espresso bar on the corner. "Can I get you something?"

"No, I never drink coffee. Do you know what coffee does to your system?"

"It's the one thing that my body responds to in a predictable way." She rummaged in a side pocket of her bag for some money.

"Maybe it's time to generate some unpredictable responses?"

"And you're just the guy to do it, right?" Claire shook her head and managed to pull a five-dollar bill free of some tissues and gum wrappers. "Talk about being predictable."

"Honey, nothing's predictable when it comes to me."

5

JASON HAD BEEN RIGHT about the college crowd.

They showed him respect, but absolutely no mercy. He reciprocated in kind.

Even at this early hour, a few dedicated members of the varsity teams—men and women—were working out. They were heavily into weight training, high rep as well as bulk. Bench pressing. Cleans. Curls. Squats. Also interval training. Running steps. Hoisting medicine balls. Contorting their bodies into Kama Sutra-type positions on giant rubber fitness balls. Sweating it out on rowing machines and Nautilus equipment.

After an hour and a half, most of the students had gone—some to classes or simply too exhausted to continue. Not Jason.

Claire wiped her brow. She had long since abandoned her anorak, and stripped down to jeans and a thin gray T-shirt with a fraying hem. To say the air in the weight room was close was a gross understatement. If someone were to bring in a truckload of snow cones, they'd melt faster than you could say "Good Humor Man," and there'd be a tidal wave of gargantuan proportions.

Trying to ignore the pool of sweat that collected in the vee front of her bra, Claire propped her foot up on a bench. She rested her elbow on her knee and focused the camera on Jason's biceps as he did curls with some humongous-looking weights. With each breath, he bent his elbows, bringing the weights to his chest, only to slowly and deliberately repeat the motion over and over. The sinews in his arms stretched taut. The muscles bunched and relaxed. Over and over. Bunched and relaxed.

She shifted the lens, focusing on his face. The intensity of his concentration as he worked, eyes shut, was hypnotic. She stared, and for one of the few times in her life, forgot to take a photo.

Jason Doyle might be a top athlete due to his extraordinary talent, but it was talent honed with an unbelievable amount of determination. Here was a man who knew the value of hard work, of pushing himself past the point of pain to what could only be more pain—all because he knew what it took to win. And that, Claire realized, was the mark of a champion. Not just the desire and the ability to make the winning shot or to score the crucial goal, but the willingness to expend the hours of solitary effort required to push the envelope of performance.

Here was athleticism in its most primitive state. Its most brutal. Its most exhausting. And at the same time, its most appealing. Its sexiest. Claire wet her lips, salty with perspiration, and took a picture.

Jason lowered the weights and stopped. He inhaled loudly, his chest expanding. The faded letters that spelled Grantham University had become difficult to read due to the drenching sweat that covered his T-shirt. Slowly, he circled his neck, loosening his shoulders. And opened his eyes.

Claire pretended to look through the camera.

"You want a go at it?" Jason motioned to the weight rack. "Your biceps look pretty fit. You must work out, too."

"My exercise comes strictly from lugging around a ton of equipment." Claire clicked a few more shots.

"Make a video and you could probably market it as a new exercise routine."

"Yeah, right. I can see it now. 'Lugging and Hauling Your Way to Fitness. Only requires twenty thousand dollars worth of camera equipment. But for a limited offer, available today only, we'll throw in a potato peeler and a julienne slicer.'"

"What, no serrated knife?" He smiled as he breathed heavily through his mouth, then peeled off his wet shirt and tossed it across the handle of a nearby exercise bike. "Boy, it's hot in here. I must have sweated off ten pounds."

Jason Doyle clothed was dangerous. Half naked, he was positively illegal. Claire didn't even bother to pretend to be taking pictures.

He noticed. And smiled wearily. "There's more where this comes from."

"I'm sure there is. But can we get back to business?" Claire hunched her shoulders and raised her camera.

Jason held up his hand, blocking the lens. "No more pictures."

She peered over the top. "No more pictures?"

"No." His voice was quiet but firm.

And it didn't seem in jest at all. Claire slowly lowered the camera. "Well, in that case, I might as well pack up and wait while you hit the showers." She chattered nervously as she straightened up.

He moved his hand to her wrist. "Why don't you not." He rubbed his thumb back and forth across the inside of her wrist.

Claire closed her eyes, telling herself she wasn't feeling the shooting spark of pleasure that penetrated every nerve ending of her body. *I will not respond*, she told herself. Then she felt him take her other wrist and double the torture.

I will not respond, she told herself again.

His fingers slid slowly up her forearms, coming to rest at her elbows. He massaged the sensitive skin, scraping his nails lightly along the crease. Claire nearly buckled at the knees. So much for not responding.

She opened her eyes. "Why are you doing this?"

"Because I want you. And because you want me."

"Maybe." Maybe? Who was she kidding? Even in deep REM sleep her body would be pulsating with desire.

But her sense of vulnerability was just as strong as her passion, if not stronger. "This is ridiculous. You can't want somebody you've only met," she protested as much to herself as to Jason. Isn't that what Trish had argued in the cab the other day? She reached out to steady herself on the bar resting on a stand behind her.

"We may have only come face-to-face yesterday, but I've known about you longer." Jason stood.

His naked torso was close, impossible for Claire to ignore. The damp swirls of hair on his chest rose and fell with each slow breath. She gripped the bar harder. "You mean, you knew about me from the spread on Clyde Allthorpe?"

"When I spoke to Trish a while back, she told me that you were the one who shot those pictures. So naturally I was curious. But I was even more intrigued when she assured me that you were the same C. Marsden whose name used to appear under photos from all sorts of godforsaken places."

Claire looked sideways to avoid his stare. "I wouldn't have thought world news was your thing, let alone noticing the photo credits."

"You'd be surprised what I notice. Every once in a while, despite my best intentions, my eye strays as I'm turning to the sports pages." She felt a finger press lightly on the tip of her chin, turning her head to face him. Her chest moved in and out as she breathed heavily.

"I'm sure you also keep close tabs on your investments." She tried to ignore the warmth of his skin against hers.

"I let Vernon deal with the financial side of things. I focus on the essentials."

"The essentials?" Claire gulped.

Jason spread his hand under her chin and gently stroked her neck with the pad of his thumb. "Six months ago I saw this photo. Some place in Eastern Europe. It was a picture of a mother, standing over a grave, her child's, and she was holding some tattered remains of a doll. Her face held no emotion, not a tear. She seemed numb. Senseless. And next to her stood a boy—her son. He was maybe fourteen—"

"Twelve," said Claire softly. Her face was blank, also. She was back there. Back in the bitter cold, among the guns, the hatred, the lack of concern for human life, any life.

Jason took Claire's chin gently in his hand and turned it up. "And he had a rifle slapped over his arm. How long was it before she stood over his grave?"

"Two days." She closed her eyes. Bit hard into her upper lip. She had been there for the second child's death, too, but she didn't take the picture. She couldn't stand behind the camera anymore and watch the destruction. Her reaction had moved beyond fear to helplessness. And that's when she had quit. Claire closed her eyes, reliving the anguish.

"I saw that picture, and I saw the credit. And I saw you." He paused. "Open your eyes, Claire."

She opened them, forcing back the tears. She would not cry. She never cried. "What you saw was a photograph, not me."

"The photograph was you—your compassion, your bravery, your humanity. I had no idea who you were, but I knew I wanted to meet you. In fact, you're not at all what I expected."

Claire looked up. "Not expected good or not expected bad?"

Jason smiled gently. "Very good. I never anticipated someone like you. Oh, I figured you'd be someone competent, more than competent. But I never figured you'd be so young, and so attractive."

He thinks I'm attractive? Claire's heart leapfrogged suddenly into the upper regions of her esophagus.

"Someone smart. Someone sassy." Jason reached over and gently placed his hand on Claire's.

She slipped it off the bar, but his hand didn't leave hers.

"Step out from behind the camera," Jason said. "Let someone share your warmth, your humor, your courage, Claire. Share your fears. With me." He lowered his head.

Claire parted her lips. "I don't know if I can. The camera is always there." Her voice was weak. She scrunched her hand by her side, but felt him envelop it with his, open it, slide his fingers around and knead away the tension.

"Trust me." He lightly brushed his lips against hers.

She shivered.

"Try." He nibbled her bottom lip with excruciating thoroughness. "Trust me. Just try."

And she did, pressing her lips to his, sinking into the

rich fullness of his mouth. She let his tongue tickle the corner of her mouth, parted her lips for him to explore further. The tip of his tongue sought out hers. They darted and mated together in a sinuous dance.

Claire didn't bother to hold back. She couldn't have even if she had wanted to. With the touch of his lips, the taste of his mouth, a torrent of emotion was set loose—anger, fear, warmth, and above all, need. It was a free fall into ecstasy, and she wasn't sure if there was any kind of safety net. And with the way she was feeling at the moment, she didn't care if there was a promise of security at the other end. Because there was no end. Only now. Him. Holding her.

Jason cupped his hands up her neck, outlined her jaw, then threaded his fingers through her hair. He moved in closer to mold his body against hers, pressing his hips against hers.

Claire felt a sharp jolt of pain. Right against the inside of her pelvis. The camera. It was digging viciously into her side. "Sh—"

Jason pulled back and looked down. "Ow. Sorry about that. Why don't we remedy the situation?" He slipped a hand under the strap, ready to lift it over Claire's head.

She saw the passion in his eyes and sensed the heat of his body. She felt her own desire ramming into her chest with a fierce intensity. An intensity that was so alien, so different, from anything that she had ever experienced before.

And it scared her out of her wits in a way that no sniper fire, no rocket attack, no minefield, had ever managed to achieve. A second ago she would have coupled with him right then and there on the floor, mindless of the fact that they were in a public place, where anyone could walk in anytime.

"No, don't." The words escaped her lips in a frightened whisper.

He stilled his hand. "Don't?"

She grasped the camera strap firmly above his hand, preventing him from lifting it away from her chest. "That's right, don't. It's not that I don't want this. I'm not stupid enough to deny that. It's just that...that...that it's too much."

"Too much good or too much bad?"

She raked an unsteady hand through her hair and ran it under her chin. "Good. Bad. Oh, I don't know. Just too much too soon."

Jason squeezed the camera strap for a second, then let go. She thought for a moment that he might touch her. But he didn't. He held his hand suspended, finally letting it drop to his side. "You may be right. Maybe it is too soon. But it's definitely not bad. That I know for sure. And I think you know it, too. So it's not a matter of it not happening. It's just a matter of when."

Jason lifted his hand again. Claire stiffened. Would he try to touch her again? She might be talking tough, but Claire knew that if he rekindled their physical contact she wouldn't stop it.

But he didn't touch her. He merely reached for his shirt and paused before turning his head to her. "I think I'm in dire need of a cold shower." He tilted his chin upward. "I don't suppose you'd care to join me? I could easily turn the heat up." His flippancy helped dispel the tension in the air.

Claire took a deep breath and felt oxygen fully enter her lungs for the first time in minutes. She couldn't call it a cleansing breath, but at least it started to moderate her blood pressure level within the upper reaches of medical safety. "No thanks, I think I'll pass."

"Well, you can't fault a guy for trying." He slung the shirt over his shoulder and walked slowly to the men's locker room. His back glistened with sweat, especially where the shallow, inward curve of his spine met the waistband of his gym shorts. A wet triangle darkened the blue synthetic material of his shorts and it disappeared into the crease of his buttocks. Even with his back turned, Jason generated more sex appeal than a rock star in spandex. Claire was just glad he was facing the other way.

She felt the urge to throw anxieties to the wind and to fling her body against his moistened torso, wrapping her legs around his lean hips, grinding her pelvis into the firm globes of his butt, and exclaiming, "Take me."

Claire looked down at herself and blinked slowly. When had she started reacting like a starstruck groupie in search of wanton sex and hazy memories? She felt the sensitive flesh at the apex of her legs spasm involuntarily. Apparently the answer was now.

"I know what you're thinking, you know," Jason called without breaking stride or looking back.

She could hear the confident laughter in his voice. She willed herself not to blush, knowing full well a rosy hue was swelling from her chest up to her cheeks like an oncoming red tide.

He couldn't possibly know, Claire thought. It was just some male mind game. Wasn't it? She exhaled through her mouth. Maybe she did need a shower, after all, and a cold one at that.

6

"WE'RE GOING TO New Jersey." Claire spoke softly into her cell phone as she sat in the lobby of the Plaza Hotel.

"New Jersey? Why on earth would you be going to New Jersey? You must be mistaken. No one goes to New Jersey, not voluntarily, anyway," Trish declared with authority from the other end of the line. "Hold on a minute, would you." It was more a statement than a question.

Claire shifted the phone to her other hand and listened to what sounded like Trish making last-minute arrangements with Elaine. Then the distinct tap-tap-tapping of four-inch stiletto heels receded rapidly into the background and Trish was back on the phone. Elaine's ability to maneuver gracefully on spiky shoes never failed to astonish Claire. She could replace a high-wire act. And where did you get shoes that deadly? Claire recalled that they looked dangerous enough to require two forms of picture ID and a twenty-four-hour waiting period from the time of purchase.

"Sorry about the interruption." Trish didn't sound sorry at all. "The meeting with the art department on next week's issue has been pushed up because the story we were running on the inside back cover has run into unexpected problems."

"Isn't that your pet-of-the-week story?" Claire seemed to remember such heart-warming stories as the snapping turtle that saved the family kitten from drowning. Or was it the other way around?

"Yes, it's what we fondly refer to as 'Furry Features.' Actually, we usually start the alliteration with another F-word, but we don't need to go into that right now. Unfortunately, it seems this week's story about a home for abandoned Akitas had to be shelved."

"Akitas?"

"You know, those big, furry dogs that were so popular several years ago. You couldn't turn around on parts of Madison Avenue without tripping over one. And believe me, you didn't want to trip over one."

Claire frowned. "I must have been out of the country for that craze. What did they do, anyway? Bite the hands that didn't feed them?" She envisioned severed arms still clutching Gucci and Louis Vuitton shopping bags.

"Seems the dogs had a little problem with incontinence. Jar their inner karma and the floodgates are likely to unleash."

"Oh-hh."

"*Oi*, is more like it. Hence the need for a shelter for abandoned pups who pooped one too many times on the Aubusson. Unfortunately, it looks like the neighbors are crying foul—"

"So to speak," Claire interrupted.

"Yes, foul." Trish carried on. "They're citing some zoning violation or something or other. And you'll never guess the place where all this is happening."

"Beverly Hills?"

"No, but close. Our own little childhood backyard."

Claire opened her mouth. "Not Leeds Springs?"

"Yes, dear, Leeds Springs, with its fashionable SUVs sporting stickers boasting the exclusivity of their children's New England prep schools and the joys of paying top dollar in Martha's Vineyard."

"In a very low-key manner of course," Claire added.

"Of course. Far be it for Leeds Springs residents to do anything crass. That would be akin to letting crab grass run amok in their perfectly manicured lawns."

"It's probably the future of the manicured lawns that concerns them, with the dogs and their little problem, I mean."

"Well, their manicured lawns are messing up my deadline. So it seems my editorial acumen is necessary to solve the crisis. That means you're on your lonesome to trail Jason all this afternoon. Poor little old you. Looking at real estate with a bachelor millionaire must be so tough. I mean, the sky's the limit—triplexes with views of Central Park, lofts in Soho, penthouses on Sutton Place."

"Yes, but he wants to go to New Jersey," Claire said, baffled. "Frankly, I can think of more exciting options."

"I can see how that might dampen your enthusiasm. Well, maybe Jason feels the need to get away from the hustle and bustle of city life. Commune with nature."

"Trish, if he wanted peace and quiet and a bit of green he could get a terrarium. No, I think there's something else going on. This is New Jersey, after all. The state that has the mosquito as its official animal."

"Is that true? Maybe we could use that for our animal story."

Claire glanced over and saw Jason stepping out of the elevator. He had changed his clothes to a pair of slate-gray trousers and a dark-blue dress shirt open at the collar. She noticed people in the lobby turn and stare. He walked in her direction, oblivious to the whispers. Claire doubted the conversations were about his collar size or the fact that his pants didn't have cuffs. "Listen, I gotta go."

"Our man has arrived?" There was a flirtatious tone to Trish's voice.

"Has he ever." Claire pretended to joke. If only she were.

"Well, call me with an update. And be careful. This is New Jersey, we're talking about."

"You mean, they have Akitas there, too?"

Jason stopped in front of her. He slipped his hands into his side vent pockets. Claire tried not to stare at his crotch, which was exactly at eye level. Then she decided why not. "The man is definitely ready," she said slyly into the phone.

"What? Details? More?" She heard Trish screech. Gone was all pretense of the jaded sophisticate.

Claire flipped the phone shut and slipped it into the side pocket of her camera bag. She smiled conspiratorially.

Jason looked puzzled. "What was that all about?"

"That was just Trish. Seems she was called into an emergency meeting at the office. She won't be able to join us on your house-hunting expedition." She rose.

Jason slipped on a pair of mirrored sunglasses and hoisted the bag off her shoulder. "Here, let me take that." Claire watched as he effortlessly swung it over his shoulder. She, on the other hand, had a permanent dent in her shoulder blade where she usually bore the brunt of its weight. He let her lead the way to the revolving front door.

"Tell me you weren't planning on driving to Jersey on that bike of yours," Claire said.

"I'm not planning on driving to Jersey on that bike of mine. Feel better?"

"Much."

"I ordered a rental car instead. It should have been delivered already." The liveried doorman nodded to them as they stood on the sidewalk under the entryway of the hotel. "Ah, there it is." Jason nodded toward the spanking-new, racing-green sports car. The prancing horse logo was unmistakable.

"That's a rental car?" Claire did a slow inspection of the car. It was all she could do not to kick the tires. "I don't see the Hertz sticker. No, of course not. Nothing to mar the paint job on a Ferrari, right?"

"Amazing what you can rent these days, isn't it?" Jason seemed mightily pleased.

Claire tore her eyes away from the gleaming hunk of metal and raw power that just about dared a driver to put it through its paces. "The motorcycle. This car. You have an undiagnosed obsession with speed and limited storage space?" she asked him.

"It is pretty, isn't it?" Jason grinned and looked appreciatively at the Italian sports car.

Claire rolled her eyes heavenward. "Pretty is not the word I would have chosen. Lunatic is more how I'd characterize renting a Ferrari for driving from Manhattan to New Jersey."

"I guess it is a little crazy. But you know boys and their toys. It must be symptomatic of a latent death wish. C'mon, get in. I can't wait to put it through its paces." She was right.

Claire hesitated. Without realizing it, Jason had touched on a real sore spot. She had had enough of the risk-seeking, adrenaline-rush lifestyle.

She used to tell herself that the reason she craved assignments in war zones and areas of natural disasters was because she was after the truth. That she felt the overwhelming need to tell a story.

What a crock. The story wasn't all that mattered. It was the high. But the high brought the inevitable low—for everybody. Indeed, the so-called high of constantly putting oneself in jeopardy wasn't brave, wasn't truth-seeking. It was selfish, plain and simple. Not being in one place for any length of time like that hurt those people who were left standing afterward. She'd been one of them—with her father, with colleagues.

"I gather from your lack of enthusiasm that you don't approve." Jason looked at her frowning face.

Claire breathed in deeply. "Let's just say I like to minimize risk as much as possible, not seek it out. How about I agree to let you drive as long as you keep to the speed limit?" She opened the passenger-side door and lowered herself into the rich leather interior. Making a deliberate show of putting on her seat belt, she turned to Jason and remarked, "'Latent?' That's a rather big word for a jock. Did you get seven hundreds on your college boards or something?" She knew she sounded catty, but he had uncovered a raw wound in her emotional makeup. And she impulsively reverted to her habitual sarcasm as a means of self-defense.

Actually, Jason had scored higher, but he didn't bother to mention it. Instead, he stashed her bag in the minuscule space behind the driver's seat and silently put on his own seat belt. He turned toward her. "You know, my grasp of the English language sometimes even surprises me."

"I'll keep that in mind the next time I suggest a game of Scrabble." She paused. "And I suppose you honed this remarkable skill at your distinguished alma mater, where you majored in—"

"Biology," he said without any fanfare.

"Biology?" Claire was surprised not only at his answer, but that he seemed determined not to rise to her bait. She was surprised enough that, despite her rude behavior induced by an advanced state of righteous indignation over the death-seeking craziness of too many people close to her, Jason remained polite. She screwed up her face and rubbed her forehead firmly. This was not good. Not good at all.

Jason put the car into first, then stopped. Slowly he returned the stick shift to neutral, pulled on the handbrake, and let the engine idle. After a moment of measured silence, he turned to Claire. "Okay, what gives?"

"Gives?"

"You know."

"I know?"

"I mean, did I do something wrong?"

"Wrong?"

"This morning? This isn't really about what happened back at the gym this morning, is it?" Jason asked.

The gym? Claire was so wrapped up in her confusion that she had completely forgotten about that whole other dilemma. God, this morning! "No, it has absolutely nothing to do with this morning." Not that she had any idea what she was going to do about this morning. At the rate she was acting now, however, the likelihood of having to make a decision in that area was rapidly fading into nothing. "Listen, I'm truly sorry about the way I acted just now. It has nothing to do with you. Unfortunately, it's my problem. I promise it won't happen again."

"Good." He shifted back into first and released the hand brake at the same time, easing the car away from the curb.

"Good? That's it? No warnings about not doing it again or I'll get twenty lashes with a wet noodle?"

"Wet noodle, huh? Sounds kind of kinky. I'll have to remember that." He smoothly shifted into second. The car glided effortlessly forward.

The traffic was heavy, but it didn't appear to bother Jason. He headed south to the Lincoln Tunnel. A stretch limousine made an aggressive move from the left lane, attempting to cut them off. He barely pressed the accelerator pedal, and the Ferrari surged forward, leaving the limo caught behind a bus that had slowed down to make a left-hand turn. The car hummed contentedly. Jason smiled. "Listen, if it makes you feel any better, when I said I majored in biology, I should have also said that my specialty was anatomy." He turned briefly in her direction. "Female anatomy." His grin widened.

Claire smiled. How ironically comforting to return to sexist banter. "You don't know how relieved that makes me feel." It was the truth. She also noted his restraint when he didn't speed up to run a yellow light. "If it makes you feel any better, I think the engine sounds wonderful."

"Yeah, it does, doesn't it?" Jason tapped the steering wheel with his fingers. "Even within the speed limit."

AFTER MORE THAN THREE hours Claire decided that the only thing more painful than looking at houses had to be a full-body search by a former East German border guard. Especially for a woman who didn't own a frying pan, let alone a stove to put it on.

When she had made the decision to return to the States, Claire knew that she needed to look for an apartment. She simply hadn't gotten around to it. Or so she told herself. For the time being, it was too easy to mooch off Trish, which wasn't fair, even if she was kicking in half the monthly co-op fee. Trish deserved her privacy, and Claire, well, she should start thinking about having more than two duffel bags and a trunk of old junk to call her own.

But there was a big difference between searching for a one-bedroom with a doorman and twenty thousand square feet of hearth and home.

When Jason had said New Jersey, she had naturally pictured landfills and oil refineries. Silly girl. Of course, New Jersey also offered rolling hills and quaint towns. And she'd known he had graduated from Grantham. Hadn't she just insulted him to his face a while back about that? Claire grimaced. So of course he knew that central New Jersey offered close proximity to New York City along with the advantages of suburban-slash-rural living.

Claire was no stranger to the mix. Leeds Springs in Westchester had offered many of the same amenities. Only the area around Grantham that they visited with the real estate agent Sandra—pronounced "S-ah-ndra" like "San Gimignano" she had informed them on first meeting—seemed less rigorously groomed and mania-cally on display. Claire found herself liking it—a reaction she never expected.

The houses that they'd seen so far were a different mat-ter. What can you say about a pseudo-Georgian mon-strosity with an indoor basketball court and circular drive large enough to park a whole battalion of tanks? Or a twenty-room modern ode to glass and brushed steel that had five hot tubs—topped only by six bidets? It was like a plumbing system on steroids.

Were these shrines to conspicuous consumption really what Jason wanted? So far he had made polite com-ments, but had shown no real enthusiasm. His low-key response was more than compensated for by the bubbly tone set by S-ah-ndra, on the other hand. Her reveries about rising local property values and the remarkable craftsmanship of the custom-made wet bars, Claire had yet to figure out what a dry bar was, was bordering on manic. What she had to say about fully finished basements with ten thousand-bottle-capacity wine cellars was positively frightening. And her delight in pointing out front-to-back entry halls rivaled the ecstasy of St. Theresa. Was it an entry or an exit hall, then? Claire wondered.

At least Sandra gushed on about the properties instead of fawning over Jason. For that, Claire was eternally grateful. In fact, Sandra made a big show out of not making a huge deal that Jason was a sports celebrity. She preferred to name-drop the CEOs of Fortune 500 companies or Nobel prize winners to whom she had sold houses. Still, Claire knew—she just knew—that Sandra was dying to ask for an autograph.

"These kitchen counters are made from a type of granite found only in Scotland, and they've been specially finished with four layers of coating." Sandra ran her hand along the stone surface in the latest monster-size house on her list. It was a crenulated, stone bastion with central air conditioning. The signet ring on her pinky helped balance the sapphire and diamond number that lavishly hid the skin up to the knuckle of her third finger.

Jason ran his hand over the counter. Claire took a picture. She could see the caption now: Hockey Star Skates Hand Across Caernarven's Cornerstone. A Man's Home Is His Castle.

"What do you think of the countertops?" he asked.

Claire lowered her camera when she realized he was talking to her. "The countertops?"

He nodded, looking perfectly serious.

Claire stopped. "Well, I'm no expert." She noticed that Sandra was glaring at her intently. She didn't want to jeopardize a potential sale. Maybe her ring wasn't completely paid off. "I think they're very hard. And very, very..." What did you say about large slabs of rock? "Very gray." Well, she had done her best.

"Yes, very gray," Jason agreed. He looked over to Sandra. "Maybe a little too gray. Perhaps there's something else on your list you'd like to show us?"

Sandra eyed Claire. "Something without gray countertops?"

Claire clasped her hands nervously "Really, any kind of countertops. I'm just the photographer." Earlier in the day, Sandra had been delighted to find out that she was a photographer. After handing Claire her card, she spent the rest of the afternoon sucking in the sides of her cheeks whenever she thought she was in view. "It's all about what Jason wants," Claire added, pointing in his direction.

"Yes, well." Sandra arched a knowing brow, and they all toddled off to her car, Jason and Claire following in Sandra's lineny wake. Miraculously, her two-piece, buff-colored linen dress refused to wrinkle, as stiff as her perfectly highlighted hair and calfless legs.

"I didn't mean to say anything bad about the countertops," Claire whispered desperately to Jason.

"They looked like petrified elephant hides," he whispered back. "Frankly, I thought you were very, very diplomatic."

"I thought maybe I'd committed some terrible real estate faux pas. Next time you want me to be the fall guy, give me a signal."

"What kind of signal?" Jason bent close to her ear.

It tingled. Claire hoped she wasn't blushing. "How

about you tug on your ear?'' She had ears on the brain. That wasn't all.

Jason smiled. She was pretty sure that he knew that wasn't all. He bent closer. "If it works for you, it works for me." He knew.

A few minutes later, as Sandra tooled them around in her Mercedes 500 series, four-door sedan in German banker black, the real estate broker turned to Jason. "Your agent, Mr. Ehrenreich, had said you preferred something new, with all the luxury appointments, but maybe there's another type of property you'd like to look at? We have a number of choice historical homes in the town of Grantham itself, and I'd be happy to show them to you. I also have several other large, custom-built homes in some gated communities that would offer you the discretion that you seek."

Claire only half-listened from the back seat. *I'm sure you'd feel more comfortable sitting next to all your equipment*, Sandra had suggested icily. It certainly was roomy, and securely nestled off on her own, in the cocoon-like bed of Mercedes leather, she could stop worrying that with an inadvertent twitch of an eyebrow, she would endanger Sandra's chance of repeat membership in the monthly million-dollar club for local real estate agents.

Her hand rested comfortably on her camera bag, and she stared absentmindedly out the window. The last overgrown pseudo-citadel they had looked at was north of Grantham. They'd reached it originally by taking the main road past the shopping center into the land of semi-secluded Adirondack bungalows and Old Money horse farms. To get back into town itself, Sandra had chosen a different route, a two-lane road that followed the path of the old canal. The channel's commercial days had long since past, and it was now part of the state park system.

Solitary canoeists and fishermen plied the waters instead of barges. Hikers, alone, in pairs, with and without dogs, walked along the towpath. Simple stone-and-clapboard houses and farms still remained next to the water or looked down from the hill gently sloping to the road. Trees leafed out over the water and dotted the landscape. It was small, intimate, Cotswolds-esque. Beatrix Potter land.

Claire immediately loved it. If she ever were to buy a house, something about as likely as fish swimming up the Empire State Building to spawn, she'd pick a spot like this—close to civilization, yet seemingly lost in time, enchanted.

"What about that house over there? There's a For Sale sign at the bottom of the drive," Claire heard Jason ask Sandra. She snapped out of her dreamworld of sitting in the garden sipping tea and eating scones with clotted cream and strawberry jam.

Sandra quickly applied the antilock disc breaks and turned up a rutted road. The sign at the bottom was partially hidden by a rather rambunctious lilac bush. Claire noticed that the listing was with another real estate agency; Sandra's cut would be sliced in two.

"The houses along the canal are quite charming, though in general they are small and many still haven't been modernized up to the standard that you are used to." Sandra could see a couple of those zeroes disappearing from the end of her commission check. "We don't have an appointment, so I'm not sure..."

"Why don't we just wing it? It's kind of neat out here, don't you think?" He turned up the charm.

Sandra dropped the hemming and hawing. "On the other hand, the possibilities are really there." Jason's high-wattage smile and aw-shucks sincerity must have had their usual effect. Or maybe she had figured half a commission was better than none.

"What do you think?" Jason swiveled his shoulders and looked at Claire.

"Wing away. I'm just the photographer."

Jason turned back to Sandra. She parked the car. "Claire's so modest. She always underplays how much I rely on her judgment. Here, let me get your door for you." He scooted out and came around to Sandra's side.

"Oh, thank you." Sandra reached for the chain strap of her Gucci bag. "Let me just go ahead and see if anyone's home so we can look inside." She stepped carefully over the loose stones.

Claire gathered up her stuff and started to open her door, but Jason got there first. "I'm not helpless, you know," she said as she swung her legs out. "I can open my own door."

"Yes, you can, and I've always admired you for that. I have nothing but healthy respect for strong, independent women."

"And I presume you owe this enlightened attitude to a particular strong, independent woman?"

"You better believe it. My mother. She ran a lumber company. Talk about tough. I learned early on not to annoy her. Besides, I owe her. She was the one who taught me how to play hockey. And to open car doors."

Claire was surprised. "I'm impressed. She sounds like someone I'd like to meet."

Jason crossed his arms. "I'm sure the feeling would be mutual." A silence fell between them. Claire shuffled her feet. This was not the time to start thinking about meeting mothers.

Jason uncrossed his arms. "You realize of course that

you've now fulfilled requirement number five for a future wife. You want to meet my mother."

"Oh, quit with this future wife requirement stuff, will you? As a long-running joke, it's really getting pretty played out."

Jason didn't say anything.

"It is a joke, isn't it? Oh, don't even bother to pretend otherwise." Claire waved her hand in disgust. "And another thing." She leaned toward him, gesturing with her finger for further emphasis. "Stop with this bit about how important my opinion is. You're just trying to make it all my fault if the sale doesn't go through."

"I'm just trying to make you a part of things."

"I don't want to be a part of things. How many times do I have to say it. I'm just the photographer." She poked his chest with each syllable of "photographer."

He looked down. "You know, without my pads, I tend to bruise easily."

"Oh, I'm sorry."

Before she could snatch her hand away, he grabbed it. "Not that I'm complaining, mind you."

"You should know that physical violence doesn't turn me on. I'm not much of an S & M girl." She tried to pull her hand away, but he wouldn't let her, playfully tugging back.

"I'm willing to make small allowances."

"That's mighty big of you. Now give the fingers back." She looked cross.

"Getting testy, are we? I tell you what, I'll let go if you answer one question."

Claire frowned. "I'm not sure I like the sound of that."

"All right. Don't answer me then. Just think about the answer. Why is it you feel the need to keep saying you're just the photographer? Hmm?" He lifted her hand and brushed her knuckles with his lips. Smiling, he looked into her eyes. Then dropped her hand and walked off, chatting away with Sandra.

Claire was left, staring down at her work boots and wondering when normal sensation would return to her hand. She was still feeling the light pressure of his lips on her skin, like the ghost response that people who have lost limbs often report. Only she felt that she had lost something more than a limb.

She shook her head. She seemed to be doing a lot of that lately and deliberately forced her attentions to the house. It was old, more than one hundred years old. That much she knew. One section was made out of stone, probably the original house. There was a two-story white-clapboard addition that was nearly as old. The glass in the multipane windows had the swirly look of handmade material, and the shutters looked as if they were actually meant to close and ward off the elements. A climbing rose trailed up over the low door of the stone portion. A weathered copper bowl filled with water sat at its base, perhaps some art trouvé kind of birdbath or the remnants of a baptismal font.

Sandra was talking with an elderly looking man who stood slightly stooped in the open doorway. He was wearing khaki trousers and one of those old-man, V-neck cardigan sweaters. He seemed a bit overwhelmed by Sandra at first, but after hearing her spiel, seemed to perk up considerably. He retreated inside the door, reappearing in a navy-blue roadster cap and accompanied by a large golden retriever. He carried a leash in his mouth. The dog, that is. Dog, leash and man bundled into an aging Volvo sedan and bumped down the driveway.

Jason signaled for Claire to come over. "Sandra has worked miracles, as usual."

Sandra blushed. "I'm just glad the gentleman finally understood that you were interested in seeing the house. Sometimes homeowners can be very funny, especially ones who have lived in a place for a long time. They know they want to sell, but they really don't like the idea. So they can be a bit touchy about having strangers come through. That's why it's so much easier when you have an appointment," Sandra said a tad critically. Only she was looking at Claire, not Jason. Now it was her fault?

"I explained it was all my fault. That I saw the sign from the road," Jason said.

Well, I'm glad that's cleared up, Claire thought.

"Anyway, turns out he was an old professor of mine from Grantham, now retired," Jason said.

"Anatomy?" Claire asked as they stepped over the stone threshold. Jason had to stoop to get through the door. They entered what was a surprisingly large kitchen, the original open hearth taking up one wall. A solid wooden table stood in the center of the room. The appliances were against one wall. Pine cabinets and cupboards surrounded a double sink. A window behind looked out over a back terrace and garden.

Sandra looked at Claire. "Any problems with the counters this time?"

"I think you've got the wrong impression about the importance I place on countertops," Claire replied only half jokingly. "In the scheme of things, I think a roof is number one, followed by a floor. Then comes plumbing and lighting. Heat if at all possible. I'm a very basic kind of gal."

Jason took Claire's arm and pulled her beyond Sandra's reach. She looked as though she might have a good right hook—Sandra that is. He had no doubt about Claire's. "Actually, the owner of the house used to teach cold war diplomacy. He said to excuse the mess." Signs of the makings of a peanut butter sandwich being interrupted were evident on the table. "His wife is away visiting their daughter in Rhode Island. Seems she just had a new baby. That's why they're selling. They want to move closer to the grandchildren."

"You learned all that in the few minutes you talked?" Claire asked.

"No, Sandra did."

"A true miracle worker," Claire said with a solemn nod.

Jason pinched her.

"Hey," she whispered. "I was being sincere."

"And I was merely flexing my fingers," he whispered back. He looked to Sandra. "Why don't we look at the rest of the house? Looks like there's a room upstairs." He pointed to the narrow staircase.

"Yes, according to the listing, there are four bedrooms, a formal dining room and living room. I suppose there and there." Sandra looked up from a photocopy of a real estate flyer that had been lying on the table and indicated the doorways to the larger part of the house and off the back by the stairs. "Oil heat, electric hot-water heater and stove. I guess there's no gas line out this way." She didn't sound impressed. "But there are ten acres of land. That's a definite bonus."

They passed through the kitchen into the dining room. The ceiling had heavy wooden beams. French doors opened to a back garden. To the left, the living room and a crowded study. Old copies of *Foreign Affairs Quarterly* lined the bookshelves. Family photos and a pipe rack competed for space on a messy wooden desk.

"These look like the original floors." Jason looked at

the wide-planked pumpkin-pine floors beneath the scattering of worn Oriental rugs.

Sandra sniffed. "Yes, I suppose so. They can be sanded and polyurethane applied, of course." She looked at Claire, waiting for a comment.

"Of course." Claire nodded, then turned away quickly before she could be drawn any further into conversation. She noticed how the limb of a dogwood dipped outside the study window, and she carefully stepped over a pile of books to take a picture.

They climbed the wooden stairs to the four bedrooms upstairs. Three were in the newer part of the house, with a large shared bathroom and a laundry room. Only one bedroom, the low-ceilinged room over the kitchen, looked currently in use. It had exposed heavy beams like downstairs and the ceiling slanted with the roofline. The double bed was unmade. The end of the quilt had a circular indentation, making Claire think the dog slept there. She sniffed. Definitely a doggy smell. Not unpleasant. Just very animally, in a companionable sort of way.

There was a window seat at a bay window looking out the back. A radio was turned on low to a classical music station. Edward Elgar's "Land of Hope and Glory" filled the room. An Elmore Leonard paperback lay open on its spine on a footrest. A pair of men's corduroy trousers, cuffed, were tossed over the back of a wooden chair. Ironed handkerchiefs were piled on a dresser, squeezed to one corner by a small TV and VCR. The clock on the VCR flashed twelve over and over.

"I see there is an adjoining bathroom." Sandra peered through an opened door. Claire walked over. It was long and narrow, just wide enough to fit a pedestal sink, claw-foot bathtub with a handheld shower nozzle, and a toilet with a wooden seat cover. She liked it and took a picture.

Jason had made very few comments as they walked through, and Claire couldn't tell if he was intrigued or not. He certainly hadn't suggested they cut the tour short, for which she was grateful. Frankly, the more she saw of the house, its coziness, its old materials and its imperfections—yes, definitely its imperfections—the more she liked it.

Liked it enough that she was seriously trying to figure out whether there would be enough to make a down payment if she cashed out her CD and mutual fund account. Now that she was on staff at *Focus,* she could probably convince a bank that she was able to make monthly payments. Not that she had any idea of what the monthly payments would be. Sandra was closely guarding the real estate report next to her immaculate self.

"The listing says there's a full basement. That's where the oil burner and tank are located. Did you want to check it out?"

"I think so. Why don't you lead the way?" Jason offered.

They headed down the stairs and discovered the door to the basement in the dining room. Sandra flicked the light switch and a single bulb turned on below. "Watch your step," she ordered as authoritatively as a nursery school teacher with twenty years' experience.

Sandra led the way, and Claire followed next. The stairs were open, and she had to hold on to the railing as they went down. Jason was close behind.

"What do you think?" He touched her on the back of her neck to get her attention. It got her attention all right. She nearly jumped out of her skin. It was good she was holding on to the railing.

What did she think? At the moment she wasn't able to recite her birth date, let alone form a cogent opinion.

Why was it that his slightest touch sent her in such a state of emotional flux that her cognitive abilities were reduced to a protoplasmic state?

"I really want to know what you feel about the house." His breath tickled the back of her neck as he bent from the higher tread.

"What I feel?" Would Sandra be discreetly professional and turn away her carefully powdered cheek while Claire threw Jason down on the basement floor and had her way with him? A potential commission was a potential commission after all.

Claire looked to the floor. "Cool, it's dirt. The basement floor still has a dirt floor."

"Yes, well, you could easily pour a concrete slab." Sandra stepped over to one wall. "It would certainly help cut down on the dampness problem they seem to have. I'd also recommend a sump pump and a dehumidifier." She pointed to some watermarks on the stone foundation walls.

"What do you think?" Jason asked.

"Hmm?" Claire was studying some old snowshoes that were strapped to one wall. Did they get enough snow around here to go snowshoeing? Or maybe the canal froze and you could skate on it in the winter. She wistfully thought of her father and Holland years ago. That memory was immediately subsumed in a more recent one—the session with Jason on the ice only yesterday. She pursed her lips.

"What do you think?" Jason repeated, coming up next to her.

Claire was remembering the kiss under the stands. His closeness now was almost unbearable. "I don't know anything about wet basements," she confided. Holding on to the railing for more than just balance, she carefully climbed up the stairs.

"I'll take it."

Claire stopped.

"What was that?" "What did you say?" Claire and Sandra asked at the same time.

"I said that I'd take it."

Stunned, Claire blinked. Then she continued on up with Jason following. They waited in the kitchen for Sandra.

Claire stared at the fixings for the peanut butter sandwich. The lid was still off the jar. She reached out and screwed it back on. She was delighted for Jason. Delighted that he saw the charm of the old place, despite not having four hot tubs—maybe especially because it didn't have four hot tubs. She was overjoyed. Really she was.

And she was disappointed. For herself.

Don't be silly. It's better this way, she told herself. What did she know about owning a house? Clearly, her comments on countertops qualified her as a home-owning menace in Sandra's eyes. And did she know anything about sump pumps or dehumidifiers? Not that she didn't have good mechanical aptitude, mind you. She simply didn't own anything vaguely mechanical other than her camera. Her beeper had died somewhere over the Atlantic Ocean, and the cell phone in her bag officially belonged to the art department of *Focus*. Heck, she was probably the only woman in North America who didn't own a hair dryer.

"Don't you want to know the price?" Sandra flicked off the basement light switch and showed Jason the flyer.

"That looks more than within my price range, even with whatever renovations will be necessary."

"Well, if you're sure, I can have a contract drawn up

immediately for your signature." Sandra knew when to seize the moment. It was a lot like potty training.

"Fine. You can just take it up with my agent. You have Vernon's number, right?"

"Of course, but if you'd like to expedite the process, we can just stop at my office in Grantham—"

"No, it'll be fine if you fax the contract to Vernon. He handles all my finances."

"If it's of any interest, I know a number of architects who would be happy to work with you, on the renovations, that is. One in particular is especially good at incorporating modern luxuries into historical homes."

"That's very kind. You can give the information to Vernon, too."

"Actually, I happen to have his card in my bag." Sandra unsnapped her purse and pulled out a Filofax stuffed with notes. "He's quite good. He put the large gaming room addition on to the first house we saw."

Claire thought back to the one she was referring to. Granted, after so many houses in so little time, it was something of a blur. But she seemed to recall a teak and dark glass house built on stilts, some misguided attempt to replicate a rainforest habitat. There had been a humongous wartlike appendage, totally out of character—all classical pediments and Chippendale cornices, postmodernism gone amuck.

The sole purpose of the addition had been to display an antique billiard table that the owner had acquired on a trip to Great Britain. The walls of the room were covered in aged wood paneling. Very Olde Worlde. Some rural Welsh pub must have been denuded of its entire interior. She thought she could still make out the holes from stray darts. Either that, or worm damage. Claire only hoped that the pub owners had demanded a stiff fee and were now contentedly living in a sunnier climate, like San Diego.

"That's okay. I don't need the name now," Jason replied hastily. Claire could tell from his lack of enthusiasm that he had had a similar less-than-positive recollection.

"No, really, it has to be here somewhere." Sandra continued to flip the pages of her date book, oblivious to Jason's disinterest. "I've worked with him many times, and the clients have always been very satisfied."

Jason looked beseechingly at Claire.

She gave him a what-do-you-want-me-to-do look.

He pulled on his ear.

She rolled her eyes. Oh, great. She was the one who was supposed to save the day, make a sworn enemy of a woman who with the snap of her fingers, could probably have the entire Junior League of Grantham hunt her down and pummel her with booklets of raffle tickets to the upcoming Designer House show.

"Ah, here it is." Sandra brandished the business card.

Jason tugged on his ear again. Violently.

All right. But you owe me, Claire mouthed silently.

With camera in hand, she did the first thing she could think of. "Jason, why don't we get a shot of you coming out your new abode, all very homey and cheery like." She stepped backward over the kitchen threshold.

"What a good idea." Jason displayed some of the lightning lateral moves he was known for on the ice and rushed out the door. A large smile, more a look of relief really, spread across his face.

The relief didn't last long.

Jason rushed out the door. Clunk. He banged his head soundly—literally—on the heavy wooden cross beam. A direct shot. Really quite impressive. Grabbing his head, he stumbled outside.

"Oh, no," Claire shouted too late. Much too late.

Still clutching his forehead, Jason blindly stepped forward. One foot landed in the copper bowl. It must be a dog dish, Claire realized at that very moment. He slipped. It clattered off the step. He tumbled down. Knocking his elbow on the stoop. Banging his knee into the stone path. Twisting his wrist at an odd angle as he went to break the fall.

Claire rushed to his side. "Are you all right?" She got down on all fours.

Jason winced. "It's a good thing they had me take the physical before I signed the contract. I'm not sure I could pass it now." He swallowed deeply, lifting his arm off the ground. He opened and closed his fist tentatively. "You know, you were the one who was supposed to be the fall guy, not me," he complained under his breath.

Claire was mortified. "I just did the first thing that came to me. I completely forgot about the low door." She reached out and feebly turned the bowl upright and patted Jason's wet pant leg.

Sandra came and stood there, looking down critically. She held another business card in her hand. "Here's the name of a local orthopedist. The way you two are going, you're going to need it a lot more than an architect."

Claire looked up and opened her mouth to speak.

Sandra cut her off. "Yes, yes, I know," she said impatiently. "You're just the photographer."

7

"I'm HAPPY to call the number of the doctor that Sandra gave us."

"Don't be ridiculous." Despite Claire's protests, he had insisted on driving the car to Grantham where they parked on a side street and went into a three-story office building. On the second floor, Jason opened the door with the sign Daniger and Fahrer, Attorneys-At-Law. Claire had this sinking feeling she was being hit with a lawsuit. Maybe that accounted for his silence on the drive here—he was figuring out how to build a case. She just hoped that *Focus* carried good liability insurance.

"Is Simone or Ted here?" he asked the middle-age woman sitting at the desk in the small reception area.

"Hello, Mr. Doyle. Ted's out with a client, but Simone is in her office. I'll just ring you through."

The door to an inner office opened within seconds, and a no-nonsense-looking woman in a black pantsuit and broad shoulders walked out. She looked at the bump blossoming on Jason's forehead. "Gee, Jason, did you get that on or off the ice?" She stood to the side and let them pass through into her office.

"Good to see you too, Simone. Simone Fahrer, Claire Marsden." Jason limped into the office and made the introductions with a wave of the hand—the one not clutching his forehead. He heaved himself down on a couch and draped one foot over the leather cushions, letting the other rest to the floor.

"Hi." Claire nodded. "Actually, I did it," she confessed.

Simone blinked. "I'm impressed. I'm not sure that I would have taken on Jason. You're obviously special. Have a seat." She motioned to one of the armchairs. She sat in the other, so they were all on the same side of the desk.

"I'm just the photographer." Claire sat and rested the bag on her lap.

"That's what she tells everyone." Jason shrugged his shoulders knowingly.

"Is that what they call it now?" Simone turned sideways to look at him.

"But I am the photographer," Claire protested.

Simone turned back. "Wait a minute. Claire Marsden. You are a photographer. A news photographer."

"That's what I've been trying to explain." Claire sighed in relief.

"And you're what passes for news these days, Jason? That's a pretty sad commentary on the state of our society."

"Glad to know I still command so much of your respect, Simone." Jason directed his attention to Claire. "Simone and I go back a long way," he explained.

Claire wondered how long and in what capacity.

"She doesn't put much stock in professional athletes."

"Only because I used to be one," Simone said.

Claire raised her eyebrows.

"I was a professional tennis player. Not that I ever achieved a level of fame close to Jason."

"Not that many people do," Jason said from the couch. "And I say that in all modesty."

"Please, I've long since become immune to your boyish charms."

Leading Claire to wonder when she hadn't. Jealousy was a terrible thing, even when it was unwanted.

"Unlike you, though, I knew that the best time to get out was when you're at the top," Simone said to Jason.

"You call what you were at 'the top'?"

Simone growled. "I can see this conversation is going nowhere." She paused. "So, to what do I owe the pleasure of your company?"

"I was house hunting."

"Anything promising?"

"Actually, I found a great old place along the canal."

"Fantastic. It'll be terrific having you close by. I'll be able to pester you on a regular basis."

Claire found herself studying the two of them, looking for little signs of sexual awareness—a knowing wink, little casual touches here and there. Subtle things, like brands on their foreheads that said, "We slept together X number of times."

Jason sighed. "She thinks because she's my best friend's wife, she has license to give me advice."

Claire relaxed her jaw. She hadn't realized that she had been clenching it.

"I don't? Ted assured me it went with the engagement ring." She looked back at Claire. "Ted is my husband and law partner. And it is a nice engagement ring, don't you think?" She held out her hand.

Claire leaned over and looked at the tasteful antique setting of tiny pearls and diamonds. "That is nice. Very fine but understated. It doesn't scream, 'I'm a high maintenance gal.'" It was much nicer than Sandra's trophy ring. "Is it an heirloom?" She looked up.

"Yes, it was my husband's grandmother's, as a matter

of fact." She studied it herself again. Smiling, she placed her hand in her lap. "I'm impressed. She has good taste, too. Not your usual type at all," she said to Jason.

"He has a usual type?" Claire asked.

"You know, arm candy. Definitely high maintenance."

"That's right, talk about me as if I weren't here," Jason said from the couch.

Claire did just that. She leaned conspiratorially to Simone. "That's very interesting. I figured that was the case. You see, Jason has told me that I have already fulfilled five of the requirements that he has for a perfect wife, and he flatly denies that it's all a farce."

Simone looked dubiously at Jason. "Five, huh? And I thought you only had three. Thirty-six, twenty-four, thirty-six."

Claire leaned back. "Well, that let's me out. Thank God I'm only the photographer, or I'd be concerned." She laughed.

No one else did.

"She says that a lot, doesn't she?" Simone said to Jason.

"Says what?" Claire asked.

"You noticed," Jason responded. He looked at Claire and shook his head.

"Hmm." Simone studied Claire, then Jason. Then Claire again.

"What?" Claire asked, confused.

Simone pressed her palms to her thighs and stood. "You know, I think it's time for me to get some ice for that bump on your head and leave you two together." She left the room, the door shutting behind her.

Claire looked at Jason. "Was it something I said?"

Jason thought a moment. "In a way."

"Care to elaborate?"

"Not really." He rubbed the back of his neck with his hand.

Claire pondered the elliptical response. Maybe she had misjudged the relationship between Jason and Simone. They had the definite conversational shorthand of long-time acquaintances, but everything—their mannerisms, the fact that she was married to his best friend—suggested they were and had always been strictly platonic friends. "You know, I was wondering at first if you and Simone had ever been an item, but then I decided that wasn't the case," she said out loud for confirmation.

Jason raised an eyebrow. "Fishing for an answer? Perhaps jealous?"

She wasn't about to admit it to him if she were. She didn't like admitting it to herself. "Curious," she clarified.

"You were jealous." He closed his eyes and smiled.

"If it makes you feel better to think that, then far be it from me to ruffle your ego," she scoffed, maybe a little too loudly. She got up and walked to the window behind Simone's desk. She looked out through the vertical blinds at the neat alley below and the back of retail buildings. No graffiti, no garbage, not even any illegally parked cars. Just a UPS truck with its engine idling.

With nothing of interest to stare at outside, she turned her attention back to the room, studying the photos, ones of Simone and a large, good-looking blond man shaking hands with various dignitaries, politicians and youthful leaders-of-tomorrow types. There was also a glossy print of a girl's basketball team sponsored by Daniger and Fahrer, grouped ceremoniously around a really ugly trophy.

And there was one that didn't quite fit the usual assortment you found in local businesses. It was of Simone, the man—clearly husband and partner Ted—and Jason. A wedding reception shot, Claire recognized immediately. They were laughing, Simone in the middle wearing a simple white dress, Ted with his arm around his new bride, and Jason holding a champagne glass. The bow tie of his tuxedo was lazily undone. His smile was just as lazy.

Damn, the guy looked sexy as hell. While there was no sign of anyone with Jason, Claire wondered if he had come with thirty-six-twenty-four-thirty-six arm candy. Then she remembered that Jason had agreed to be Trish's arm candy at the wedding this coming weekend. She turned away. She didn't want to think about it.

She circled around the desk and leaned against the front edge. She picked up a small stuffed toy of a tiger. It was loosely filled with beans. She started fiddling with it, squishing its stomach. It was very squishable. Addictively so. "The funny thing is when I saw you were taking me into law offices after the accident with your head and everything," Claire said casually to Jason, "I was worried you were considering suing me and the magazine for personal damages."

Jason opened one eye. "What makes you think I'm not?"

"It looked like your relation with Simone was more personal than professional."

"Ah, you're still jealous."

Claire rolled her eyes. She set the tiger back on the desk but continued to poke at it, positioning its paws in different ways. "That's not what I mean, and you know it."

"If you say so."

"Argh." She breathed in deeply.

"You know the idea of seeking some kind of remuneration for bodily assault isn't completely unappealing."

"Please, you make so much money, whatever you'd get out of me and the magazine would barely keep you in cupcakes for a month."

"Cupcakes for a month? That has a certain appeal. What flavor?"

Claire looked at him sternly.

Jason tilted his chin up and squinted. "Actually, I think I've figured out how we could settle the damages in an appropriate manner."

Claire depressed her thumb into the tiger, giving it a large inny belly button. "You have?"

"Yes, I have." He lowered his jaw and looked at her. "I'm sure that if you kissed it where it hurts, it would make it a lot better."

Claire made a face. "You're not serious?"

"No, I am," he said perfectly sincerely. "And really, when you think about it, it's a small price to pay for jeopardizing the career of a star athlete."

"Please, you haven't jeopardized your career."

He looked at her askance.

Claire hesitated. "Just a kiss, right?"

He nodded. "It will make all the difference."

She thought about it. "Okay, just a kiss, if you're sure."

"I'm sure. But you'll have to let go of the death grip on that tiger. Simone wouldn't like to come back and find it decapitated. She's very fond of tigers. She married Ted after all."

Claire reluctantly let go of the toy. "And I suppose you're not a tiger?"

"No, I'm a pussycat."

"Even cats have claws."

"I've retracted mine, see?" He held up his fingers. "Why don't you come over here and administer to the wounded?" He patted the couch cushion.

She pushed herself off the desk and walked over to the couch. "As long as I don't have to don some Florence Nightingale outfit, I guess it's all right." She looked down at him.

"What? No nurse's uniform? A little role-playing could spice things up."

"Are you looking to sustain additional injuries?"

"And here I was hoping that you'd be a fun girl." Jason tried to sound disappointed.

"I am a fun girl." Was she? So much of her efforts had been spent on doing her job in terrible conditions and simply staying alive. More times than not, fun had come down to a hot shower or a big chocolate bar with hazelnuts.

Not that she hadn't had a few relationships here and there. But her peripatetic lifestyle and the type of men she usually came in contact with meant these relationships had never panned out into anything serious. They tended to dissolve by mutual consent, a quick flame fed by the threat of desperation and dowsed just as quickly. Claire had never bothered to ponder who was tossing water on the fire. Thinking about it now, she realized that she'd always been the one leading the bucket brigade. Occupational hazard, she rationalized in retrospect. Coward, she thought more truthfully.

But she was fun, wasn't she? The people she took pictures of responded to her humor and relaxed with her easy banter. But without the camera? Could people still respond to her? Could Jason?

She walked over and sat on the edge of the couch. "Where does it hurt?"

Jason held up his arm. "Here." He pointed to his elbow.

Claire studied the brown streak on the sleeve. "That

looks more like dirt. Maybe the dry cleaner would do a better job than me."

"Trust me, you're a lot cuter."

Claire thought of the dry cleaner on the corner by Trish's apartment, and decided it didn't take much to be cuter. Nevertheless, her heart did a little pitter-patter.

"And it's not just the shirt. It's the bone, right here." He indicated a spot above the elbow and moved his body closer to the back of the couch to give Claire more room.

Claire inched over. She leaned forward. "You sure you want me to kiss it?"

"That's right. Right there. Didn't your mother ever give you a kiss when you fell down and hurt yourself?"

"Are you kidding me? It would have been distasteful to her and embarrassing to me."

"Frankly, that's all a little strange. But at least you won't be drawing on any maternal instincts when you kiss me. And I really don't want you having any maternal thoughts, believe me." He propped his bent elbow on his other hand and waited.

Claire stretched out her neck and kissed it lightly. She kept her eyes open and looked at him while she did it. He looked at her. "Okay. Anywhere else?" she asked.

"Here." He pointed to his wrist.

She moved her head and kissed that lightly, too. This time his skin was exposed and she could smell the intoxicating scent of soap, dirt and pure Jason Doyle. She shakily lifted her lips. "Does that feel better?"

He lowered his arm, never shifting his gaze from her. "Better." He rested his hand on her thigh.

She thought of moving, but didn't. This time she wasn't going to run away.

"But there's more," he said.

She gulped. "More?"

He nodded to his shoulder.

She inched closer and kissed it through his shirt. She stared at the open neck of his collar.

"And here." He indicated the bump on his head.

"Yes, that's a particularly bad one, isn't it?" She leaned forward, letting her hand press gently against his chest. Her lips lingered on his forehead. She closed her eyes briefly and playfully rubbed her nose across the thick locks of his hair that had fallen forward.

"And here," he said softly. His breath rumbled against the exposed skin of her neck as he spoke. Claire shivered. She forced herself to pull back to see where he was indicating. She didn't want to break contact.

His lips were slightly parted. His flecked brown eyes had turned almost black with desire. "Here," he said, pointing to his mouth.

She leaned even closer. His hand pressed harder into her thigh. The weight was driving her wild. "Here?" she whispered, her lips barely separated from his.

And then they weren't separated at all. His mouth was on hers, around hers, tasting, searching. No. That was hers on his, tasting, searching. She clenched her hand on his chest, gripping the material in her fingers.

He pulled back slightly. She felt disappointed. Was it over? "Feel better?" she managed to say between breaths. See, she could be fun.

"Much better." His breathing was just as ragged as hers. "But I still need more."

"More?"

"More." He squeezed her thigh and removed his hand.

She wanted to put it back. But then she felt it on her hand on his chest. He loosened her fingers and raised her hand to his shoulder. He wrapped his arm around her back and pulled her near. "I want more. Much more," he repeated.

They kissed, deeply, lips parting, tongues dancing. Claire dug her fingers into his back. She opened her mouth more. He let her explore him. And she did. And he did so in return.

He leaned back on the couch, pulling her on top of him. His hand skimmed under the hem of her sweater. She quivered as his fingers roamed the small of her back and moved farther up. She arched her spine, pressing her breasts into his chest, her nipples sensitized through the layers of clothing.

"Sorry it took so long to get the ice, but the delicatessen next door was crowded—" Simone stopped. Her hand was still on the door where she had just opened it.

They sprang apart. Claire sat up swiftly, quickly checking to see that she still had all the necessary body parts, let alone the right pieces of clothing covering them. She patted her hair and stole a glance at Jason. He was straightening his collar. Both feet were planted less than surely on the ground.

"Claire was checking out my bruises," he explained.

"Was she now?" Simone walked deliberately across the room. She didn't bother to hide the grin on her face. "Funny how the temperature in the office seems to have gone up suddenly. Maybe I should have brought more?" She held a plastic bag of ice toward Jason but looked at Claire when she asked the question.

"Thanks." Jason took the ice and placed it on his forehead. He winced when the cold hit his skin.

"You sure that's where you need it?" Simone asked.

Claire looked down.

Jason shifted awkwardly on the couch. His arousal was pressing against his pants. "Maybe we should get going? I've got an appointment back in the city later." His voice was tighter than usual.

"I just bet you do." Simone leaned back against the desk. She crossed her feet at the ankles. "Ted will be sorry he missed you."

"Well, we're sure to catch up. He was coming in this week anyway, right?"

"That's right. We'll see you at dinner. And we can find out more about your new house." She tapped the toe of her dress loafer. "And you'll be there?" She looked at Claire.

Claire slipped the lock of gray hair behind her ear. "Me? Unless it has something to do with the magazine, I don't think so. I'm just the photographer." She stood and walked to gather up her camera bag.

Simone uncrossed her feet and stood. She slowly turned to Jason. "She says that a lot, doesn't she?"

8

"OH, MY GOD, Jason, what happened?" Trish looked at the bruise. "You didn't hit him, did you, Claire?"

"Why do you suppose it was my fault?" Claire walked over to the large picture window in Trish's office and plunked her camera bag on top of the heating vent. It wasn't on, so she didn't need to worry. Actually, it was never on. *Focus*'s editorial offices had two options. You could have a window with no heat or a windowless cubicle with heat up the wazoo. Since windows were a coveted mark of prestige, the senior staff kept their precious views and a ready supply of last year's pashminas in their credenzas.

Claire looked down at the idling traffic on Broadway. She turned back and crossed her arms.

"It was just an accident. My fault," Jason said. "And it's nothing. Nothing at all. There's no need to give Claire a hard time." He certainly hadn't given her a hard time during the drive north to Manhattan. In fact, he hadn't given her any time at all.

After their soul-searing clinch on the couch, Jason had turned decidedly mute. Conversation in the car had been reduced to comments on the weather—"Warmer than I would have expected for this time of year"—to the traffic—"Don't you wonder why so many people are on the highway in the middle of the day?"—to movies—"I usually wait till they come out on video. I just get hassled too much if I go out." Claire supposed she was lucky that they hadn't sunk to asking each other their astrological signs.

Not that she felt any more comfortable about the whole scene on the couch. What was supposed to have been a spur of the moment plunge into unencumbered lust, now seemed to be a suicidal swan dive into an emotional maelstrom. She had been anticipating a sensory jolt—heck, her hormones had been doing a jitterbug since first encountering Jason Doyle. But there was no way she could have expected every nerve ending, every patch of skin, every multifunctioning organ, every eyelash, to go totally topsy-turvy, only to crash and burn, and start the process all over again. Even now, she wasn't sure whether to call the fire department or to simply will her body to medical science immediately.

And from the way Jason's hands had repeatedly clenched and unclenched the steering wheel, and the way he'd hunched his shoulders into a rigid comma as he drove, she guessed his chi wasn't exactly in a peaceful state, either. What she wouldn't give for a CD of ocean waves and wind pipes. For both of them.

"Regardless of the blame, there must be something I can do to make it better." Trish's voice interrupted Claire's failed attempt at meditation.

"That's what got us into some of our trouble," Claire mumbled.

Jason looked over.

"What's that?" Trish buzzed her intercom. "Elaine, are you there? Elaine, will you get us three double skim lattes?" She turned to Jason. "Jason, please sit down. Take the couch. Stretch out."

Jason held up his hand. "That's all right. I'll just take the chair." He lowered himself carefully into the Mission-style armchair that Trish had picked up antiquing in the Berkshires the summer before. She had felt the sudden urge for style and comfort after she had misguidedly agreed to an invitation from an oboist performing at Tanglewood. She had always heard that oboists went crazy from blowing those double reeds, but she hadn't really considered the exact meaning of crazy until he had suggested sleeping on rush mats and flaying each other with fly swatters. To make matters worse, the swatters looked used—from flies that is.

Trish waited until Elaine brought in the coffees and left the office before she spoke. She was sitting behind her desk, and played with her ergonomically designed pen—her latest toy. She peered at Jason closely, then swiveled around toward Claire.

Claire was clutching her coffee cup with two hands and trying not to think of couches.

"Well, I suppose you can touch up any photos, right?" Trish asked.

"You're concerned about the photos?"

"Why? Should I be worried about something else?"

Claire opened her mouth, then closed it. "What happened with your Akita crisis?"

"Ah-h-h. Being evasive there. So I *should* be concerned about something else." She set her pen down. "Never mind. I'll get to the bottom of that later. As to your question, yours truly came up with a brilliant solution—a story about how all these insensitive neighbors are threatening the very existence of these abandoned, cuddly dogs who have done wonderful things, including visiting old people in rest homes. The old people were a particularly nice touch."

"Do they make pot holders in their spare time, too?" Claire blew on her coffee. So far, the heat had singed her fingertips while she was waiting to drink it. "The dogs, not the old people."

"Not that I know of, but I am sure they could if they wanted to," Trish said. She picked up her latte and took a large gulp. Editors didn't appear to have any problem with consuming hot liquids. They could probably make pot holders, too.

"Akitas? Aren't they the dogs that pee all over the place when they get nervous?" Jason asked. He put his coffee cup on Trish's desk.

"That's an unfortunate reputation that the dogs have acquired, and I'm sure it's totally undeserved."

"I don't see you rescuing one," Claire said.

"Yes, well, my lifestyle doesn't include a dog at the moment. But I'm sure if it did, I would consider getting one immediately."

"It's the thought of all those pot holders."

"Enough of the pot holders." Trish beamed a high-wattage smile on Jason and shrugged her shoulders. Her open-weave, boat-necked cardigan slipped off one shoulder. Did the woman own nothing that stayed in place? It had bits of colored ribbon worked into the nubby blue-black thread. Maybe she was losing it, but it seriously reminded Claire of a pot holder. "Well, bruises and all, I am extremely happy that Claire brought you back in one piece. Tomorrow, we have a full day sched-uled, and I have cleared my calendar to spend it with you."

"I'm honored." Jason didn't seem too pained at the idea.

"It also gives us the chance to start to 'go public,' so to speak."

"Oh, that's right. The two of us as an item." Jason made a motion with his finger.

"You aren't having second thoughts, are you?"

"No, I gave my word."

Trish sat back, pressing her hands against the table. She arched her back to stare over her shoulder at Claire. "He gave his word. Isn't that the greatest?"

Claire couldn't help noticing that Trish's dark-blue demi-cup bra was clearly outlined through her sweater as she held that pose. She was sure that Jason noticed, too. "The greatest."

She brought the coffee cup close to her mouth and sipped. It had gone from boiling hot to lukewarm without an intermediary stage. All this manpower and money put into building stealth bombers and nuclear submarines. What the world really needed to achieve universal peace was a cup of coffee that would stay at the right temperature.

"See? High praise from Claire, and she never has anything nice to say about anyone." Trish leaned forward again to give her full attention to Jason. This time, the front of her sweater gaped open. Did the woman have no shame? From the way Jason's eyes had suddenly grown very large, apparently not. Maybe the world didn't need the perfect cup of coffee, but merely enough semifrontal exposure to rob men of any capacity to wage war, let alone anything else.

"You make me sound like I'm no fun at all," Claire interrupted. Her most recent attempt at having fun had not exactly been a rip-roaring success.

"No, it's precisely because you do make such acerbic comments about people that you are fun," Trish responded but kept her attention on Jason. "Now enough about Claire, and more about you. We're going to shoot you all around the city tomorrow, doing all sorts of touristy things—Central Park, Empire State Building, the windows at Tiffany's. And I'll be right there, having fun with my number one man. And, Claire, I want you to record all the gory details. Especially the gory details." Trish pulled up her sweater. It slipped back down again, even farther.

"I didn't think *Focus* was that kind of magazine," Claire said.

"It isn't. Those photos will be strictly for me." Trish winked.

Claire rubbed her head and reminded herself that Trish really was her best friend, even if she did act like an idiot sometimes. Besides, all this recording of lovey-dovey moments was part of the fake-fiancé plot that she had thought up. Trish was just following the script. So there was no reason for her to be irritated. But she was.

Talk about acting like an idiot.

"Well, be sure to save a few for me, as well." Jason turned his full-wattage smile on Trish. Claire felt like gagging.

"Maybe I should save a few other things?" Trish didn't bother pushing up her sweater this time.

Jason's eyebrows rose. "I'll keep that in mind."

Claire pushed away from the wall and stood. "As fascinating as this is, I really must be going."

Jason looked at his watch. "Me, too, unfortunately. I have an appointment with Vernon. It looks like we're finally closing in on the endorsement package. And now that I've found a house, I want him to get moving on that as quickly as possible."

Trish's intercom buzzed. "Excuse me," she said. She picked up the phone and spoke into the receiver.

Claire slung her bag over her shoulder and walked around the desk. "You really have an appointment?" she asked in a low voice.

"Yeah, what did you think?" he asked.

"That it was some kind of excuse to give Simone."

"You think we needed an excuse?"

Claire bit her lip. "You're right." Of course he was right. Talk about an awkward situation.

True, it wasn't as if he had been an unwilling party in the embrace. It's just that, given her impromptu decision to abandon all inhibitions, she had let things progress beyond what she initially intended to happen—for him, as well, it seemed. Well, what had happened, happened. At least she could be adult enough to move on and reestablish their professional relationship.

"About earlier today on the couch."

"Concerning what happened back at Simone's office."

They spoke at once. She coughed. He rubbed his nose.

"You."

"No, you."

Trish looked up, putting her hand over the receiver. "Sorry, this won't take long."

Claire and Jason waited. They looked at the floor, at Jason's full coffee cup on Trish's desk, and reluctantly, at each other.

"Listen, I don't want you to feel awkward about this afternoon." Jason looked down and spoke under his breath so that only Claire could hear.

"I don't. Well, yes, I do," Claire whispered back. "I'm not sure what happened, but since we're going to have to work together the rest of the week and through this weekend, maybe we should just try to forget the whole thing?"

Jason looked at her out of the corner of his eye. "You think you can?"

"Of course. I'm a professional. We're all professional, here to do a job, help a friend." She nodded at Trish.

Trish chose that moment to look up. "Hold on a sec, please," she said into the phone. "Listen, you two." She switched her attention to the room. "This looks as if it's going to take a few minutes, and I don't want to keep you waiting. We'll see each other tomorrow as scheduled? I'll send a car around to pick you up. I can't wait."

"Sounds good," Jason said. "Just one question. About the wedding—do I need to bring a gift?"

"Bring a gift. That's very sweet. He is sweet, isn't he?" she said to Claire.

"The sweetest. A regular Hershey bar." Claire nodded.

Trish laughed. "That was such a Claire-thing to say." She reached across the desk and put her hand on Jason's sleeve. Claire flinched. Jason didn't. "Don't worry."

"I'm not worried. I would have had Vernon arrange something."

"Would that we all had a Vernon," Claire said. "Does he do windows, too?"

"No, but I'm sure he can arrange to have them done."

"A man after my own heart." Trish sighed. "Listen, don't bother yourself or Vernon over the wedding. You're doing enough as it is. I haven't figured out what to get them yet, but I will."

"Aren't they listed at Marshall Fields or Saks?" Claire asked. "You can get them twelve cut-crystal water glasses, or whatever young newlyweds are asking for these days."

"Claire, as you well know, they are not so young—especially the bride-to-be."

Claire blinked. "And she says I'm the one who makes snide comments?"

"I have an excuse. I'm the one who was spurned. But not anymore, right?" She patted Jason's shirt but didn't remove her hand. She looked at Claire. "And I suppose you've already gotten them the matching finger bowls?"

"I'm providing the free wedding photos, remember?"

"That's right. How could I have forgotten?"

A voice sounded through the phone.

"Whoops," Trish said to all concerned. "Got to go."

"Well, good luck with the shopping," Claire called as she went out the door. She didn't want to wait and have to share an elevator with Jason.

"Thanks," Trish called out. "Come to think of it, I may have something in mind already."

THE NEXT DAY, Trish had a lot of things in mind. And Claire had to record it all. The ride through Central Park was obligatory. "That's right. Cuddle up together," Claire instructed, sitting opposite in the hansom cab. Jason ad-libbed, putting his arm around Trish. "Good, that's good." She concentrated on focusing the camera.

Trish turned her head and kissed Jason's cheek.

"Maybe a little too obvious," Claire said, looking in the viewfinder.

"I don't know. Seems like a good idea to me." Jason snuggled even closer and gave Trish a loud kiss on the lips.

Claire looked down and rummaged through her bag. "That's okay, guys. You can break apart. I need a new roll of film."

The horse snorted.

"ISN'T THAT JUST ADORABLE, Claire?"

"Adorable," Claire begrudgingly admitted. She could probably count on one hand—no, one finger—the number of times she had used that adjective before today. And she was proud of that record.

Well, records were meant to be broken.

Normally it would have been hard to imagine a large, lumbering—no, Jason Doyle was far from lumbering—hunk of a guy looking adorable. Not on a shopping spree at FAO Schwarz's toy store. The multistory retail icon for children's playthings had a way of making grown men behave like little boys.

Not that Jason was out of control. He was tremendously serious about having a good time. "I'm an uncle. I've got a niece and a nephew. I take my duties seriously." He sure did, questioning mothers and their children about what was the latest thing for seven-year-old boys and kindergarten-age girls, and then enthusiastically trying out the toys.

Claire got some great shots of him on the ground testing out remote-controlled cars along with a boy from Mamaroneck. And his close examination of the cloth dolls verged on the hilarious. "Do you know why they all seem to have striped stockings?" he asked, holding one up to the camera.

"Not a clue, but could you lose the cap?" Jason was wearing a Blades baseball cap, and Claire didn't like the shadows it was casting indoors.

He doffed it, ruffling his hair in a manner that would have taken a stylist forty-five minutes and two spray cans of mousse. He looked around for a place to put the hat then tossed it to Claire. She stuffed it into her camera bag, and he went back to examining the doll with a critical eye, lifting the skirt as he did so.

"Hey, put that down. No hanky-panky here." Claire laughed from the other side of the camera.

He looked up and blushed. She took the picture. He looked at the camera. No, he was looking at her. She lowered the camera. She felt a hot flush rise from beneath her turtleneck and rise to her face. All she was thinking of was hanky-panky.

"Don't you just love it? It's so humanizing," Trish cooed in her ear.

Humanizing?

"What little girl wouldn't want you for an uncle?" Trish called to Jason. "Hey, let me get a closer look at those dolls." She sauntered over and bent her head over the doll that Jason was holding. The tinkling of her laughter wafted beyond the display like Chanel No. 5 at a perfume counter.

Claire pursed her lips. Jason as an uncle wasn't exactly what she'd been thinking. She dug into one of the pockets of her cargo pants and pulled out a stick of gum. She peeled back the wrapper—Trish held up another doll next to her cheek—and jammed the gum into her mouth.

"Isn't it cute?" Trish snuggled the pigtailed doll.

"Adorable." Claire chomped on her gum. Twice in one day she'd used that word. Actually, the doll was kind of cute, but that was beside the point, especially as Trish pretended to walk it along Jason's arm. Not knowing how to react, she raised the camera. And took the picture. Jason turned and picked up another doll. He seemed to be asking Trish's opinion. Then he turned and picked up another.

Claire noticed the way Jason's jeans cupped his taut butt as he moved back and forth. "Adorable," she murmured, bit harder on the chewing gum, and did what she always did—took the picture.

A few minutes later Trish proudly carried a shopping bag from a sales counter. She stopped next to Claire and pulled out one of the striped-socked dolls. "I can't believe I got one. Whatever you do, don't tell anyone at the office that I bought one. My image as a jaded sophisticate will be ruined."

Claire surveyed Trish's getup—red leather pants, four-inch-heeled sandals, and teeny-tiny black sweater that would barely fit the limp-limbed doll dangling from her hand. Her fine blond hair was almost falling out of its low chignon. True sophistication lay in the work it took to get the "almost" look.

"I don't think there's any danger of you disappearing from the pantheon of Manhattan trend-setters," Claire said, noticing as she spoke that Jason appeared to be the one signing the credit card slip. A true sophisticate, it seemed, also knew how to gain results with some well-timed oohs and aahs.

Claire didn't ooh and aah. Adorable might be creeping in to her vocabulary, but ooh and aah would never make it. Jason came up next to her. "I didn't get you a doll."

"That's all right. I'm not exactly the doll type."

"I didn't think so." Jason pulled a small bag out of his jacket pocket. "Here."

Claire smiled stiffly. "You shouldn't have."

"I know. I just wanted you to be eternally grateful." Jason pushed the present toward her.

"Well, if you put it that way." She took the bag, and reached in, pulling out a key chain. She looked closely. A plush gorilla hung from the end of the chain.

"It reminded me of you," he said.

Claire played with the gorilla, hooking its thumb in its mouth. It looked pretty silly. "Thanks. I think." She looked up. "What exactly about it reminded you of me?"

"Hey, that's cute, in a really goofy sort of way." Trish leaned to get a better view. That meant she was also leaning against Jason. Claire tried hard not to notice. Yeah, right. "You can put your keys on it," Trish said.

Claire pulled the gorilla's thumb out of its mouth. It didn't look quite as ridiculous that way. "Actually, I think he looks very capable, in a gorilla sort of way," she said, defending her new friend. She patted its stomach protectively. It was rounded but firm, a body that was clearly strong but not sculpted by the rigors of step aerobics. She could relate to that. In truth, if Claire ever took the time to notice her body as she toweled off from a shower, she would have seen that the cumulative effect of working tough assignments under rough conditions had left her stomach not only hard, but flat. But perception, as they say, is all, especially when it comes to a woman's evaluation of her own body.

"No, I think I'll hook it to the outside of my camera bag," Claire said. And she did just that, fastening it to the tab on a zipper. "He can keep me company on those long flights around the world." She flipped it and smiled.

"Silly, Claire, you don't need to do those flights anymore. You're here in New York."

Trish latched on to the sleeve of Jason's leather jacket. "Shall we hit the next location. I have some great ideas."

Jason swung his shopping bag of toys toward the elevator. "Lead the way." And like all sophisticated couples wearing leather and carrying large bags of toys, they looked...well, they looked extremely couplelike.

Adorable, Claire thought.

CLAIRE BIT DOWN so hard on her gum that she just about cracked a tooth at Tiffany's.

There was something extremely stressful about looking at engagement rings with a minimum price tag of forty thousand dollars. Especially when Trish was doing the looking.

The shots that they'd planned for *Focus* had gone without a hitch. Naturally, the glamorous jewelry store was delighted to have the free publicity, and Trish's idea to have Jason eating a Danish à la *Breakfast at Tiffany's* was corny but worked.

It was all the other stuff that didn't play well, at least as far as the future health of Claire's dental work.

First came the close study of china patterns and flatware. "It'll give me ideas of what to get for the wedding," Trish said. Claire knew she was talking about this weekend, but the saleswoman would have had to be a clairvoyant not to assume that it was for Trish and Jason's supposed plans. Yes, Claire reminded herself, this was part of the plan. But did Trish really need to make such a big deal about having Jason decide between Spode "Evening Twilight" and Royal Doulton "Scheherazade"? And why did it irritate her so much to hear after much discussion they were in total agreement that the Cristofle dinner knives had just the right weight?

Claire picked up one, noticed the price tag, and put it down quickly. She could practically fly to Jamaica and back for the same price. A food bank could easily stay in business for a week.

It's not that she didn't appreciate beautiful things or deny people the right to buy them. It's just that they had never seemed important to her. And stupidly, naively, she had assumed they didn't mean anything to Jason, either. But why would she assume a super-rich jock, who was used to renting fast cars and no doubt, fast women, would yearn for the simpler things in life? Was the old stone house in the country just an impulse?

Claire rubbed her jaw. Her brain was wandering, and if she weren't careful, she'd lose it when it came to the choice of demitasse spoons.

She hoisted her camera into place and took a picture.

But it was almost too much at the ring counter. As she watched Trish slip on different rings, have her finger measured, listen to the salesman, and discuss the four Cs—carat, color, cut and clarity—Claire felt like an intruder. And when Jason held the tips of Trish's fingers to examine one square-cut mega-weight specimen, she wanted to turn tail and run. Any more intimate a scene and they'd all be in bed together asking, "Was it good for you?"

A shiver ran up Claire's spine. Her jaw was sure to start showing signs of bone decay. And her stomach seemed to have decided that last night's take-out Moo Shoo pork was rematerializing as a hidden dragon. She had to do something before total body meltdown took place.

She leaned closer to the duo. "Trish, I think we probably have enough pictures for the scrapbook. David will get the idea, trust me."

Trish fluttered her fingers and watched the diamond sparkle. She swiveled her neck around. "But it's kind of fun," she whispered.

"Fun is fun, Trish. It's time to wrap it up. Lunch beckons." The thought of lunch elevated Claire's stomach into a crouching tiger position. She breathed in deeply. "Trish, it's not fair to the salesman." Claire nodded in his direction. He was discreetly rearranging rings on the velvet-covered display.

"Don't worry. Picking an engagement ring can be a long, drawn-out process."

Claire snapped her fingers by Trish's ear. "Earth to Trish. You're not really engaged. Doesn't the whole charade bother you a little? Does it occur to you that as soon as you leave, someone who works here, having recognized Jason, might just rush to the phone and call the tabloids, no matter how much discretion they maintain?"

"Gosh, I hope someone is doing it now and not bothering to wait. I'm dying to see tomorrow's papers."

"Doesn't this bother you?" Claire looked at Jason.

"It's not like I'm involved with anyone else," he said.

Claire felt a sudden aerial kick to the solar plexus.

"There're rumors about my love life appearing all the time."

"But this isn't true," she protested.

Trish turned around. Hands on hips, she studied her. "Claire, after all this time, and as someone in the business, you can't tell me that you think what's written in the newspaper is true?"

"It's what I've always striven for."

Trish patted her on the shoulder with her left hand. "And we love you for that, we really do. Don't we Jason?" She sighed.

Claire swallowed. She looked at Jason. Waited. Wondered. And kicked herself for wondering.

He opened his mouth to speak.

"Don't worry. That was merely a rhetorical question." Trish reluctantly removed the ring and turned back to the counter. "I'll have to think about it. But thank you," she said to the salesman.

Claire looked at Jason. "She meant she really didn't want an answer."

But Claire did.

Jason scowled. "Don't worry. Us jocks know what rhetorical means."

9

CLAIRE DIDN'T THINK it was possible to feel any worse. First, overwhelming jealousy consumed her. Then, total embarrassment that she had sounded so condescending when she was only trying to cover her own nervousness.

She saw Vernon waiting for them outside Lutèce. That's when she decided that things could still get worse. From the way Jason greeted his agent—the chin-nod-grunt-one-shake-handshake routine—she could tell the visit was expected. From Trish's frosty hello and limp handshake, it wasn't. Pete Rose showed more enthusiasm greeting the commissioner of baseball. My, my. Fun and games over a three-star French meal.

They settled into a square table in the corner of the garden room, the women sitting across from each other, likewise the men. The waiter appeared, and Vernon took command like Admiral Perry at the helm. Claire shifted in her chair. If the tone of the conversation didn't alter soon, it would soon degenerate into seven years before the mast.

"Would you like anything from the bar? Lunch is my treat of course." Vernon spread his hands.

Claire breathed in deeply. "How about a bicarbonate?"

"Oh, Claire, that's such a film noir thing." Trish put her napkin on her lap. "Since you're paying, Vernon, I'll have champagne."

"Good idea, champagne for the table." Vernon discussed the various vintages with the sommelier, and turned back to the others when the delicate negotiations were complete. "So." He crossed his arms in front of his well-toned chest. For someone who did not naturally have broad shoulders, his tailor and personal trainer were to be congratulated.

"So." Trish planted her elbows on the table and clasped her hands under her chin. The large piece of quartzite encapsulating her left wrist slid down as if on cue.

"I presume you guessed my presence here is not accidental," Vernon said casually.

"I don't believe in accidents. Do you, Claire?" Trish looked at her friend.

"Well, it depends on the accident." Claire played with the rows of forks in her place setting. Having just sampled the wares at Tiffany's, she could attest to their quality.

"I told Vernon where we were eating," Jason spoke up. "I thought it would be the best place to talk."

"If you have some problems with the magazine story, you could have called me at the office." Trish straightened her shoulders, stretching her teeny-tiny sweater a point just short of snapping. Amazing the tensile strength of these new fabrics. "And before you say anything, you should know that Claire is doing an absolutely fantastic job."

"Yes, so Jason has let me know." Vernon nodded.

"You did?" Claire turned to her right and asked.

Jason brushed a speck of nothing off the white tablecloth. "Well, it's the truth."

"To tell you the truth, it's not the article that concerns

me," Vernon went on. He waited to elaborate as the sommelier arrived with the champagne.

Claire leaned toward Jason and whispered, "I want to thank you for not telling Vernon about the accident." She pointed to her head. "You know?"

He waved off her comment. "Vernon is my agent, not my keeper. I don't tell him everything."

"It's to do with this wedding thing," Vernon announced after tasting the champagne and declaring it acceptable. "I have to tell you, I've got problems with it."

Trish waited for all the drinks to be poured. "What do you mean, this wedding thing?"

Claire wasn't thinking about the wedding. She was still consumed with the idea that Jason had lavished praise on her. That he hadn't blabbed about her causing him to conk himself on the noggin. It also appeared that he hadn't spread tales about their tussle on the couch. She breathed a sigh of relief and felt more confident than she'd felt all day. Maybe she had judged his reaction incorrectly. Maybe he was just as shaken as she had been, and that had been his reason for retreating so suddenly. "I think that's a good thing," she ventured. "That you don't tell him everything, I mean."

"No need to be coy, Trish," Vernon continued. "Jason confided about the arrangements this weekend. I can completely understand the awkwardness of attending a wedding of an ex."

"You can?" Trish asked.

"Excuse me, are you ready to order yet?" The waiter rematerialized at the table. Claire hadn't even gotten around to opening her menu. She was stuck in that nervous state of debating "he likes me, he likes me not, no, he possibly really likes me after all, or maybe—"

Jason opened his menu for the first time.

Trish closed hers with a snap. "Why don't we have the prix fixe lunch all around? As long as you're splurging." She smiled at Vernon.

Vernon looked at her, not at all perturbed. "Why not? I'll order the wines to go with the meal then." Almost as an afterthought he turned to Jason and Claire. "That's all right by you?"

Claire held up her hands. "Hey, I never question the person paying the bill."

"I have him pick out what clothes I wear in the morning, too," Jason deadpanned.

"And what a nice job you do of wearing those clothes." Trish winked at Jason. She gave him the full wattage of her smile. She turned back to Vernon, the charm gone. "Now, you were telling me what an awkward position I'm going to be in this weekend."

Jason leaned over to Claire. "He doesn't really dress me. That was sarcasm."

"Yes, even us photographers know what sarcasm is. Listen—" She placed her hand on Jason's to emphasize what she was trying to say, realized what she was doing, and quickly removed it. She put it in her lap and bunched up her fingers. What a stupid thing to do—this predilection she had for touching him. She felt nervous. Ridiculously so. "Listen, I didn't mean to imply before that you didn't know what rhetorical means. In fact, I can't even remember what I meant at the time. But whatever I meant, it wasn't that. I mean, I'm sure you know what rhetorical means." She paused. "Am I making any sense here at all?"

He reached under the table and pried her clenched fist apart. "It's okay." He spoke softly so that only she could hear.

"So you can understand why it's so important?" Trish leaned toward Vernon.

"Absolutely. Two years ago I had to attend my ex-wife's second marriage. I never would have gone if my daughter hadn't insisted. The divorce had been amicable as these things go."

"I'm sure," Trish agreed.

"You're sure?" Claire grimaced.

Jason nodded, squeezed her hand reassuringly, then let go. She wanted it back in his.

"But it was still a big thing for me to come to the wedding. Her new husband is a nice guy, but I felt like a third wheel. Basically, unwanted. I stayed as short a time as politely possible, without disappointing my daughter. Would you like to see her picture?" Vernon reached for his wallet.

"Of the wedding?" Trish sounded alarmed.

Vernon laughed. "No, my daughter." He pulled out a wallet-size photo.

"I'd love to." Trish took the picture, glanced at it briefly. "Isn't she lovely? Don't you think, Claire?" She passed it across the table.

Claire studied the picture, a school portrait photo of a young girl, probably nine or ten years old, all nose and bangs—Vernon without the hair gel. Her mouth worked hard at firm sophistication, but the corners still curled up with a childlike impishness. "She shows a lot of promise." She liked that the smile still managed to eek its way in there.

"Bread anyone?" Jason uncovered the rolls in the middle of the table.

"So you understand why I need Jason to keep his promise?" Trish shook her head no-thank-you to Jason.

"Yes, please." Vernon took a roll and placed it on his

bread plate. "It's just that I can't agree with Jason doing this."

Claire passed the photo to Jason.

"Thanks, I've seen it. Cute kid," he said.

She held it out for Vernon.

Jason pointed the breadbasket in her direction.

"No thanks," she responded.

"Why on earth not?" Trish asked. She looked at Claire.

"Because I'm not hungry," she answered. What she really wanted was a chance to talk to Jason, but the conversation seemed to be going in too many other directions. At a loss for how to continue, she sipped the champagne. "It's delicious," she complimented Vernon.

He nodded without bothering to try it. "It's a very good year." He focused intently on Trish. "Right now we're involved in some very important endorsement negotiations. How would it look if my client—the image of mom and apple pie—turns out to be masquerading as somebody's fiancé, just to seek some revenge against an ex?"

Jason shook his head. "Me? Mom and apple pie? For a thirty-two-year-old single man, that's a little depressing."

Trish grasped the stem of her champagne glass. "But it's not revenge."

But he was mom and apple pie. He was also a hell of a lot more. Claire took another sip. And another. "What do you want it to be? Sex on the hoof?"

"You and I know it's not revenge, but what will the average Joe think? I don't want to risk it."

"Sex on the hoof? Not bad. What do you think?"

"I think you're crazy to think there's any risk. Who's going to say anything?"

"It's not a question of what I think." Claire felt a little

dizzy. She really shouldn't drink in the middle of the day, especially on an empty stomach. "Maybe I will have some bread, after all." Claire held out her hand. It was shaking a little. By accident, she brushed the top edge of her champagne glass. It wobbled.

"Can you be sure of that?" Vernon asked.

Jason shot out his hand and righted Claire's glass. "Steady there."

"Who's going to say anything? I certainly have nothing to gain. Jason? He doesn't even know anyone to say anything. Claire? She's just the photographer."

Claire looked at Jason's strong fingers surrounding her glass. "Nice reflexes." She imagined those reflexes doing things to her, too.

"Right, Claire?" Trish leaned across the table. "Right?"

Claire put the roll slowly on her bread plate. "What was that? That I'm just the photographer? That's what I keep trying to tell everybody."

"Still, I'd feel a lot better if I could monitor the situation," Vernon said earnestly.

"You keep saying that." Jason offered her butter.

"I know that sometimes I'm a bit of a control freak," Vernon answered.

Trish stopped her champagne glass in midair. "Aren't we all to a certain degree?"

Claire took a curl of butter.

"I wasn't talking to Vernon," Jason said to her.

"Would you feel better if you were there in person?" Trish asked.

"I'm not sure I know what you mean," Claire said.

"Absolutely. There's only one catch," Vernon said.

"Why am I not convinced of that?" Jason firmly cupped the top of her glass with his hand.

Trish waved his concerns off. "Don't worry. I've already thought of that. Control freak, you know."

"What?" Claire asked.

"What?" Vernon asked.

"You'll come as Claire's date."

Jason turned his head abruptly to Trish. "What?"

Claire stopped blinking. "What?"

"It's simple really." Trish leaned back, pleased. "Jason will come as my fiancé and Vernon will come as Claire's date."

"But I didn't say I was bringing anyone," Claire said.

"Don't worry. One more place setting isn't going to make a difference. Vernon can just sit at our table. You're going to be running around anyway, taking pictures."

Claire sat back and crossed her arms over her chest. "That's right, I'm just—"

"Don't say it." Jason eyed her, then Vernon. "I don't need someone snooping around."

Claire looked at him with bewilderment. "But I am—"

"This could work." Vernon nodded and appeared to relax.

"And Vernon can just share Claire's room," Trish suggested.

"Now wait a minute. If I want to go away for the weekend with a woman, I'll do it on my own. It's not like I need somebody doing a bed check." Jason loomed over the table toward Vernon. His hand lurched in the opposite direction. The champagne glass, which he had been so firmly grasping, tipped. It knocked on the table, spilled its contents, rolled against Claire's soupspoon and dessertspoon, meandered to the side of the table, and dived over the edge.

Jason's lightning reflexes never came into play. He was still fuming at Vernon.

Claire's heart sank at Jason's words. And her insecurities marched to the forefront. So he was planning on sleeping with Trish. She lowered her head and watched the delicate flute bounce off the floor, hit again and shatter.

CLAIRE EXCUSED HERSELF from the table and went to the ladies' room to try to repair some of the damage caused by the spilled champagne. She was mopping up the hem of her turtleneck sweater when Trish opened the door.

"Are you all right?" Trish pulled a few more paper towels from the dispenser and held them out to Claire. "Well, at least it doesn't show that much on black."

Claire stopped patting her front and looked down. "That's okay for the sweater. Somehow it doesn't work for the pants."

"No, it doesn't." They both looked at the dark stain on Claire's olive cargo pants. It covered part of the top of one thigh and edged conspicuously into her crotch. "Who'd have thought one flute could hold so much champagne." Trish inspected the damage closely.

"Yes, who'd have thought?" Claire blotted a few more times and gave up. "I guess I just wasn't meant for fine dining."

"Don't be ridiculous. It was an accident. Jason feels awful."

"About as awful as being forced to have his agent baby-sit him over the weekend." Claire looked at herself in the mirror. In the light, her gray streak looked bigger than ever. She sighed. At least she wasn't trying on bathing suits.

"Don't worry. Vernon will straighten that out." She looked in the mirror, too. Propping her Fendi bag on the counter, she reached in and pulled out a lipstick, expertly applying the deep plum color to her lips. She looked over at Claire and held the tube in her direction.

Claire shook her head. "I'd probably do further damage." She pulled her sweater down as far as it would go, but that only seemed to emphasize the stain at her crotch. "You know, as long as we're done for the day, I might just bag out of lunch. I feel somewhat inappropriately attired, and I'd really like to get into the darkroom to start developing all this stuff. You wanted prints for the wedding, right?"

Trish frowned. "I hate to see you miss out. We could try wrapping a tablecloth around your waist. You know, the pareo effect? You could start a whole new trend in restaurant attire."

Claire laughed. "You could start a whole new trend, Trish. Not me." She pulled the schedule from a back pocket of her pants. "It looks like tomorrow is an awards dinner at the Waldorf."

"Yes, I'm going, too. Vernon suggested it. I'll sit next to Jason on the dais." Trish looked at the mirror and smacked her lips, distributing the lipstick evenly. She scraped a fingernail at the crease and turned to Claire. "Not such a bad prospect when you think about it."

Claire looked at her over the top of the schedule. "Even when you don't think about it." She folded the sheet of paper. "You sure you need me? A ton of sports photographers will be there. You can just buy something from the Associated Press."

"Don't be ridiculous. There's a Claire Marsden photograph, and then there's the rest of the world."

Claire sighed. She could have used some space from Jason and this whole charade—or what seemed like not such a charade after all. What was all that touching and confidential chatter between the two of them at the table all about? Had she totally misread his signals? Was he really planning on maximizing his options? Playing it both ways? Claire shuddered. Jason was a celebrity used to getting what he wanted, but she hadn't credited him being that self-centered. Maybe she had been naive to believe that his mom-and-apple-pie image was real.

"Ah, it's tough to be wanted by so many people," Claire mocked, as much about Jason's desirability as about her professional worth. "Let me retrieve my bag and offer my regrets. Then I'm out of here. And about tonight—I'll probably be out pretty late. I've got a ton of film to process."

She went back to the dining room and explained she was leaving.

Jason rose—damn it, why did he have to be so polite? "I can't believe my clumsiness."

"Don't give it a thought." She hoisted her camera bag to her shoulder.

"I can't help it. Can I buy you a new set of clothes?"

"Don't be ridiculous. It's not like they're new. Anyway, I'll just throw them in the wash."

"No, let the cleaning lady," Trish interrupted.

"Nonsense. Send it around to my office. We'll take care of it. I won't even take it as a tax write-off," Vernon said.

Claire had to get out of here as quickly as possible. The only thing more painful than fending off Jason's apologies was contemplating the IRS. She offered her swift goodbyes, and adjourned, neatly avoiding the waiter and the first course.

She balanced her bag against her hip and pushed open the heavy door. The restaurant was housed in a brownstone constructed when doors were built substantially, a symbol of wealth rather than a deterrent against crime. She pulled her turtleneck close to her chin. Autumn in

New York had a tendency to turn a bit nippy in the late afternoon.

Focus's offices were on the other side of town, but Claire decided to forgo a taxi and hoof it. As she headed west, the breeze bit through the weave of her sweater, causing the wet areas to cool down quickly. Her hands immediately started to lose heat and the tips of her fingers grew numb. She wondered if she had a scarf buried at the bottom of her bag, and stopped to rest it on one bent thigh. Unhooking the top closure, Claire stuck her hand in and rummaged to the bottom. She hit pay dirt. Only it wasn't a scarf. It was Jason's Blades cap.

Just her luck. Well, a short detour to the Plaza wasn't that much out of her way, a bunch of blocks north, then the zigzag south. Besides, she couldn't get any colder, and the walk was actually helping to clear her mind. Or so she told herself.

What did she want in a relationship anyway? Hypothetically thinking of course. Of course. Security. Trust. Respect. Companionship. All admirable, universal wants and needs.

But what about love?

What she felt for Jason was definitely lust. Yet she also craved security, trust, respect and companionship from him, as well. If you combined all those things with lust, what was she really talking about?

Claire was not the type of person to use the L-word. In fact, she couldn't remember if it had ever played a role in her life. She had idolized and respected her father's talent and energy. But he was too self-absorbed, too unaware of his role as a father to offer her a loving relationship. They had never been Dad and Daughter, but Big Jim and Clair-y, adventurers like Tom Sawyer and Huck Finn. And her mother? Claire wrinkled her nose. There was definitely a match not made in heaven. She didn't resent her mother, she just felt a lack of connection with her. She sometimes wondered if she had been abandoned by the gypsies on her mother's doorstep, only to be taken in as this week's socially acceptable charitable cause.

Yes, that was the right analogy. Claire was a charitable cause for her mother. But unfortunately, she didn't provide an opportunity for black-tie fundraisers or tax exemptions. Maybe she could discuss the latter with Vernon.

So what did she feel for Jason Doyle? Claire was afraid it was something more than simple lust. But what did she plan to do about it?

Claire fingered the brim of his cap. Oh, God, she had never been a coward. But then, she had never been this unsure of herself, either. Should she reveal her feelings to him? Or was the prospect of rejection too difficult to bear? No, the prospect of defining her feelings was what really scared her.

In any case, it was not as if she had to solve the meaning of life today. She could bury herself in the darkroom, and hopefully come to some kind of decision by tomorrow's dinner. No, the weekend wedding was more than enough time, she told herself. Who knew, by then things between Trish and Jason could be so hot and heavy that her emotional to-and-fro-ing would be irrelevant. The two of them were made for each other. She had thought so the other morning at the Garden, and whatever muddled feelings she had right now were just that—muddled.

She strode purposely up Fifth Avenue past St. Patrick's Cathedral and crossed over near the Museum of Modern Art. As usual, taxis were jostling for position in front of the Plaza Hotel, and Claire sidestepped the luggage racks carrying a generous selection of Louis Vuitton suit-cases and overstuffed garment bags.

She went through the heavy revolving doors into the spacious lobby and marched across the thick carpet to the desk clerk. Strategically placed mirrors and intimate lighting assured that the high-paying clientele looked spectacular, in that Vaseline-lens kind of way. Marlene Dietrich would have approved.

The clerk looked up from the desk, his slicked-back hair as glossy as the finish on his ballpoint pen. "Can I help you?" He slipped the pen into the breast pocket of his well-tailored uniform jacket.

Claire undid the top of her bag and pulled out Jason's cap. "Yes, I have to return something to one of the guests at the hotel." She put the hat on the counter, carefully avoiding contact with a vase of orange gladioli, never her favorite color or flower. "It belongs to Jason Doyle."

"I'm sorry. You must be mistaken." The man went on to deny Jason's presence at the hotel.

Claire waved him off. "Don't worry. I'm not some crazed fan. I'm working with him on a story for *Focus Magazine.* And it's not like I need to see him or anything." She waggled the cap. "He left this at today's shoot. Honest. I'm just the photographer."

"No, she's not."

10

THE DESK CLERK REACHED for the phone. "Should I get security, Mr. Doyle?"

Jason glanced at the young man. "No, it's all right. She's a friend of mine. I just wasn't expecting her." He turned to Claire. "I thought you were going back to work?"

"I—I was," she sputtered. "It's just that I realized that I had your hat by mistake. So I thought I'd drop it off on my way. Here." She shoved it in his direction.

He took his hands out of his jacket pockets. "Thanks."

Claire looked everywhere but at Jason. "So, I guess I'll be off now." She stepped around him. "See you tomorrow night." She waved.

Jason put out a hand and grabbed her arm. "Wait."

Claire waited.

Jason frowned.

"Yes?" She started to look around for an escape.

"The thing is, the thing is..." Jason groped for the right words.

"You're starting to cut off circulation." Claire nodded to her upper arm.

"Oh, sorry." Jason let his hand drop. It inadvertently brushed the front of her sweater. "Jeez, you're soaked. You shouldn't walk around like that in this weather."

Claire looked down. "Don't be silly. A little water and cold weather never hurt anyone."

"Someone should have told that to Shackleton. You're coming with me and borrowing a shirt."

"Don't be ridiculous."

"Would you rather I have—" Jason looked over at the desk clerk, whose head swiveled back and forth as he closely followed the exchange. "What is your name?"

"Randolph, sir."

Jason eyed Claire. "Would you rather I have Randolph here call Bergdorf's and order you a cashmere sweater set in teal?"

"You're crazy."

"Maybe teal isn't right for your hair color. I think cranberry suits you better."

"What's with you? Outside of an L.L. Bean catalog, nobody uses words like teal and cranberry."

"Well, your options are teal and cranberry or a plain gray T-shirt, washed but not pressed."

Claire rolled her eyes.

Randolph looked from Jason to Claire and back to Jason again.

"All right." Claire heaved her shoulders. "I'll take the T-shirt."

Jason smiled. He looked to the desk clerk, who seemed a beat behind.

"Oh, oh, yes." Randolph stepped away. "Just a moment."

Claire shifted her bag to her other shoulder. "This is completely unnecessary, you know."

"Indulge me. I'm a star after all."

Claire snorted softly. More like a snuffle. "I hate to tell you, but you don't really seem like the overindulged athlete."

"Tell that to Vernon. After you left, I pulled a star-athlete temper tantrum and stormed out of the restaurant. That, coupled with the way I blew up earlier qualifies as overindulged athlete behavior in my book."

Claire's mouth dropped open. "You really did all that?"

Jason opened his mouth and nodded. "Yes."

"No."

"Your key." Randolph returned. "There's also a message for you from a Mr. Vernon Ehrenreich."

"Thanks." Jason grabbed the key and the pink slip of paper. He ushered Claire toward the elevator. She practically tripped over her feet.

"I can't believe you did that. The temper tantrum bit." Her mouth was still open as he bundled her into the elevator. "You've done it before?"

The doors shut before anyone could enter. "Never."

"That's what I thought."

"Am I that obvious as a goody-goody?" He stood in the corner and spread his arms out on either side, resting them on the brass railing. His leather bomber jacket fell open. His shirt lay unbuttoned at the neck. His dark brown hair tumbled carelessly over his forehead. The scar on his cheek stood out prominently against his five o'clock shadow, and the small curved one by his eye cupped the outside corner in rakish fashion. He was breathing through his open mouth. His chest rose and fell. He looked wild. And the wild look was most evident in his eyes, which were almost coal black. And they were focused on her.

There was no mistaking desire.

Claire gulped. "How would you define goody-goody?"

He pushed away from the corner and planted a leg on either side of her.

"Don't you think you should push a button for your floor?" Claire watched him move close.

He leaned across and stretched out his arm to press a button on the panel behind her. He left it there, enveloping her.

Nervous, she started to stand back. No, you don't, you coward, she told herself. She took a chance. "Why did you storm out of the restaurant?" Claire ventured. "Did it have something to do with me?"

He studied her face. "I didn't like the idea of Vernon shacking up with you over the weekend."

She shrugged her shoulders. "We're hardly going to be shacking up. Just sharing a room."

"Too close." He put his other arm on her shoulder and slipped off her camera bag. It banged to the floor. He eased it away with his foot.

"But there'll be twin beds."

He bent his head. "I don't care if he sleeps in a bathtub. As long as it's in somebody else's room."

"Somebody else's?"

"Yup." He stepped closer. Lowered his head.

"And why is that?"

"Because I intend on sharing a bed with you, that's why." He kissed her on the neck. Soft. Warm. Almost ticklish.

Claire let her head fall to the side. She gulped deliberately. "What about Trish?"

He took advantage of the length of exposed skin and ran a trail of light kisses up her neck and under her chin. "Trish? You want her there?" His voice was husky.

Claire closed her eyes. "No, I don't want her there. Do you?"

He readjusted his stance and removed his hand from the wall. He cupped her jaw with his strong hands. "At the risk of forgoing every man's fantasy—no." His lips moved to feather kisses on her eyes, her nose. "Claire, open your eyes."

She did slowly. "How did you know I'd be here?" She waited expectantly.

"I didn't. I was planning on going over to the magazine and laying on my full dosage of charm."

"Of which you have a great deal."

Jason cocked his head. "You think so?"

"Please, you know so."

His grin became positively wolfish. "My plan was to beguile you so much that you'd have no choice but to agree to come back with me to my hotel." He circled his head to the side.

"And then when I came back to the hotel, what next?" Claire circled hers to the other.

He recircled. A snake charmer's dance. "Why, we'd talk about the weather."

"The weather, huh?" She reached up and nipped him on the earlobe.

He breathed in sharply. "I'd bring up the problems caused by holes in the ozone layer, thus impressing you with my knowledge." He traced his fingers up her face, outlining the contours of her cheekbones.

"I'm impressed, I'm impressed."

He smiled. "Then I'd tell you how much I liked your hair. Your gray streak really turns me on." He put his face close to the side of her head and breathed in deeply.

"My hair? Is that all?" She felt her eyes closing again.

"That's not all," he said. "I'd tell you how much I liked your eyes, your nose, your lips. And of course you'd say the same things about me."

She opened her eyes and grinned. They both had these positively dopey looks on their faces. "Oh, would I?"

"You bet—because I'd be using my full dosage of charm. And then eventually, after I waited a suitable length of time, I'd hold you close."

"Like this?" Claire placed her hands on the back of his head and rose up on tiptoes.

"Yeah, something like that. Only I'd kind of lean down." He angled his head.

"Jason?" she whispered.

"Yes." He was closer.

She locked her fingers in his hair. "You don't have to wait any longer."

"You sure?" He studied her face.

"I'm sure. Kiss me before I explode."

And he did.

There wasn't anything sweet about it. It was pure need. Long overdue need. His mouth captured hers. His tongue explored at will. They bit, nipped, dove into each other's mouths. Tasting, taking, sharing.

Claire lost all sense of time and place. She was overwhelmed by the pure essence of Jason. His smell—vaguely citrusy and all male. His feel—strong, confident, welcoming. His taste—slightly sweet from the champagne and something indefinably Jason. Intoxicating.

She wrapped her body fiercely against his. Rubbed her legs up against his. His hands raced up and down her back. His hips pressed against her waist, the evidence of his arousal already apparent.

The elevator stopped with a small jolt. They rocked, startled. Still holding each other, their heads came apart.

Jason looked up as the door slid open. "I'm not positive, but I think the earth just moved."

She rested her head on his chest. "I knew you were a man of many talents, but what can I say?"

He rubbed his chin back and forth across the top of her head. "It's a team effort, you know." He stilled, pulling his head back. "You want to come inside and play some more?"

"I'd be crazy not to." Actually, she did feel pretty crazy right now. Crazy but not completely out of control. She looked up. "We should talk." She put her hand on his chest.

He took it in his and kissed the fingertips. "Do you really want to?" The door slid shut again. He bent and kissed her with aching gentleness. He lifted his head away and waited.

"When you put it like that—" She kissed him in reply.

In a giddy blur, he hit the elevator door button and they tumbled into the hall. Kissing, touching, stumbling, they made it to his door. He fumbled with the key card, his awkward attempts punctuated with kisses.

The door gave way. They fell inside, spinning around like drunken sailors, ripping at each other's clothes. His jacket went flying. Her sweater lifted up over her head. Her hands feverishly worked the buttons of his shirt. He yanked it off, popping the buttons on the cuffs. Breathing heavily, his hands slid up and down her slender sides, slowing only to cup and mold her breasts through her bra.

"I need you naked," he gasped. He pinched her nipples through the black lace. She gasped. He pulled at the hooks. The bra dropped. Somewhere. Their lips locked together again. Their shuffled feet interlocked, tripping over each other, half falling on a couch, half falling off.

"Not exactly great teamwork," Claire said, momentarily coming up for air.

Jason nuzzled her behind the ear. She sighed. His hand

moved to her breast, circling, rubbing the pad of his thumb over the taut point. She moaned.

"Oh, I don't know about that," he said, lowering his head and feasting on her breast. He traced the rounded underside and teased the nipple with his tongue and teeth. Her hips bucked up, grinding into his. His mouth switched to the other breast and repeated the arousing torment. She was spiraling. Out of control. Completely.

One minute she was drowning—blissfully, mind you—under the weight of his body. The next she was weightless. He had swooped her off the couch and was carrying her.

"What...what are you doing?" she stammered, looking around, barely registering the furniture in the living room suite, only half noticing the discarded clothes on the floor as he stepped over them.

"Something novel." He kicked open the bedroom door. "I'm taking you to a bed." He walked swiftly, purposely, a man on a mission, with more than the missionary position in mind. "Do you mind?"

"Mind? Why should I mind?"

Holding her against him with one arm, he strode to the king-size bed, bent and pulled off the spread. Pillows went slipping and sliding. He gripped her tighter.

Claire watched all the activity happening around her. "I can see where that weight training comes in handy."

He laid her out on the cool sheets. They smelled freshly ironed. "I always have a higher purpose in mind."

"Always?"

"When it comes to you, I am extremely focused. Now, I think I said something about getting naked." He reached down. Claire moved to undo the snap at her waistband. "No, my turn," he said.

Jason circled her waist with his hands. Slowly, he

slipped one inside her waistband. Pop. The snap came undone. He lowered the other hand. Eased down the zipper, and with both hands, peeled her pants over her hips, exposing her black bikini underpants. His lips parted. He placed his hand on the rising mound and gently pressed with the heel of his palm.

She inhaled sharply.

He looked up. "See, good things come to those who wait," he said.

She put her hand on top of his. "Don't wait."

He didn't. He twisted around, quickly unlaced her boots, yanking off her socks and pulling down her pants. He kicked off his loafers. Struggled with a sock. And won. She sat up and worked his pants button and zipper. She pulled at his pants, but he didn't wait. Couldn't. He stood up. Pushed them down, stomping on the legs hurriedly. He tossed aside his boxers.

And stood there naked. Absolutely glorious. The muscles of his body strong, defined, tense. His erection jutting toward her—strong, defined, tense. Claire blinked. "Wow."

He stepped closer, his bulging thighs pressing against the edge of the mattress. The light spray of hair curled against the crisp sheets. "Like what you see?"

Claire shook her head slowly. She hardly had the words to describe how much she liked it. "Pretty sweet," was all she could come up with.

He chuckled. His penis bobbed. She licked her lips. He gulped. "Well, you were the one who said I was a regular Hershey bar." His voice was tight.

Claire looked at him. Mesmerized. "That's right. I did. And you know what?" She reached over and pulled him down next to her on the bed. She ran her fingers through the curls of his chest, continuing the journey between his rib cage, along the indentation of his stomach. His abdominal muscles jumped under her touch. She circled his belly button, scraping the nail of her index finger along the edge. And she went lower, tracing the line where springy, dark pubic hair met skin. He quivered. She murmured.

"What's that?" His voice was barely a whisper, each syllable coming with a heavy breath.

"I'm ready to take a bite. That's what's that." She scooted up on her knees and brought her face down, brushing the tight curls with her face, breathing in his musky scent. She reached for the rounded globes behind his fiercely erect penis and gently cupped them. He hissed. She lowered her head. Her tongue traced a line up the tight, smooth skin of his penis, stroking slowly to the head. When she reached the throbbing tip, she opened wider, taking him inside her mouth.

"Oh, Claire." His hips lifted involuntarily off the mattress. His hands came down quickly, raggedly working his fingers through her hair. His head thrashed back and forth on the pillow. And then he was dragging her up. "I can't take any more. I'll explode. I need to be inside of you when that happens."

He reached over to the nightstand and yanked open the drawer, holding her at the same time. A box of condoms fell out. The packets slithered onto the carpet. He hastily picked one up, letting go of her flesh to rip open the foil. His hands were shaking. "I bought them after that first day at the rink. I hoped I'd get lucky." He struggled to open the packet.

"Trust me. Luck has nothing to do with it." Still sitting astride him, she reached down to help. And found her hands were shaking, too.

Somehow they opened the condom. Somehow got it on

him. Somehow she lowered slowly—achingly slowly—on him. Savoring the stretching, the burning, the rapture. He grabbed her waist. Moved her up and down. She closed her eyes, moved of her own accord. Slowly. Her mouth fell open. They moved together faster. Sweat pooled on her body. His was slick, too. She was growing tight, pulsating. He reached to where their bodies pounded into each other. His finger found her sensitive nub. He massaged it and pounded harder.

She shattered, screaming.

And then she was flying—no, rolling. Her back on the sheet, now damp from his body, and he was on top. She opened her eyes, saw the passion in his, the strain on his face. He kissed her cheeks, her eyes, her mouth. The taste of him on her lips mingled between the two of them. She closed her eyes. And felt his throbbing still within her, still straining.

He shifted his hips. He raised his buttocks until only the tip of his penis was still encased in her. She cried out. She couldn't stand being separated. She reached up. Pulled him down. And started climaxing all over again. And through the spasms he stroked again. Hard. She exploded, biting her fingernails into his sides, anything to get a grip on the sensations that were sending her to a realm of pleasure beyond anything she could control. He plunged again. She didn't even bother to struggle for control. The desire for control ceased to exist. Only desire consumed her now. He plunged one last time. And exploded, too, calling out her name.

Moments later he gradually shifted his weight, placing his hands on either side of her body. He straightened his arms and hoisted his chest off hers. It was not without difficulty.

Claire cleared her throat deliberately. What had she

done? *Just had the most fantastic sex ever*, the small part of her brain that was still functioning immediately answered back. She exhaled loudly.

"I know exactly how you feel." Jason balanced on one hand and combed his hair off his forehead with his fingers.

Claire looked at his face, his amazingly handsome face. "Do you?" If so, she could use some enlightenment.

Jason squinted. "Is this one of those trick questions?"

Claire frowned. "No tricks. See." She held up her hands. "Nothing up my sleeves." She rotated them for inspection. "No sleeves in fact."

Jason ducked his head and nipped her on the shoulder. "And just the way I like sleeves—nonexistent." He licked her skin where his teeth had left faint marks. "Hmm. Salty. I wonder why?"

"I seem to remember exerting a little physical effort."

He raised an eyebrow. "Only a little?"

Claire shrugged. "Well, maybe more than a little."

"So, you'd compare it to running a marathon?" He shifted his attentions to the inside of her elbow, nipping and licking. "Yes, definitely salty."

Claire opened her mouth but the words weren't immediately forthcoming. "Marathon? No, I don't think it was anything like a marathon."

He lifted her limp arm and kissed the inside of her wrist and her palm. "What about swimming the English Channel."

Claire inhaled sharply as he sucked lightly on the tips of each finger. "The English Channel?"

"Yes, the English Channel. The body of water separating England from France." He lowered her arm to the bed and concentrated on tasting her collarbone. Then moved to doing incredible things between her breasts.

She practically whimpered when he shifted his attentions to her ribs below. He lifted his head. "Oh, did I miss something?" He placed his mouth on the tip of one nipple, sucked gently, then did the same to the other. He brought them to firm, dusky peaks before ceasing his labors. "You didn't answer me, about the English Channel."

Claire wanted to laugh but all she could do was gasp. "How can you talk about bodies of water at a time like this?" She hoisted herself up on her elbows and looked at him.

"But I'm fascinated with bodies, especially yours." He moved his attentions lower, dipping his tongue into her belly button. "Yes, definitely salty, but trace elements of something else I can't quite place. I need to explore further." He grinned at her. "The Southern Hemisphere beckons."

She collapsed with laughter. But stopped abruptly when his mouth trapped the soft folds of skin between her legs. Within seconds, she didn't even know her own address let alone the geography south of the Tropic of Capricorn.

SHE TURNED HER HEAD on the pillow. The light filtering through the sheer curtains was already growing dim. Sex in the afternoon. She could really get used to it. Sex in the evening, night or morning for that matter.

The problem was, it really was getting to be evening, and she really had to get some work done. "Please don't take this personally, but I absolutely have to go to the darkroom. It's this assignment I've been on. I've had to traipse around the city, taking all these pictures of this superjock. Problem is, now I have to start developing the stuff."

Jason folded an arm on the pillow and propped his head on it. "Problem? Doesn't sound like much of a problem. Tagging along after a star athlete. Sounds pretty exciting to me."

She turned and looked at him. "I guess if you're into that sort of thing."

He looked at her. "And are you?"

She grinned. "What do you think?"

"I think answering a question with a question is a copout. But judging by your recent actions, I'll assume it means yes."

"My, my. It's always a treat to meet a man with a healthy ego."

Jason rolled over onto his side and faced her. The sheet was draped around his waist, exposing his muscled chest. Claire stared at the mat of hair that sprinkled across his upper torso and tapered into a fine line, ending below the edge of the sheet. And she knew just where.

"Believe me, my ego is not the healthiest thing about me," he said.

Claire raised an eyebrow. She grabbed the sheet and lifted it. "You're right." Sighing, she dropped it back into place. "Unfortunately, duty calls." She swung her legs to the side and started to get up, suddenly realizing she was naked. Well, at least the dimness of the room would lend a certain mystery to the details of her body. She squared her shoulders and rose quickly. "Do you mind if I use it?" She pointed to the bathroom, and walked as quickly as possible, picking up her discarded bra and panties on the way.

When she came out, Jason was sitting up in bed. She looked around, found her jeans by the side of the bed, and headed to the living room to pick up her sweater.

"That's still wet, isn't it?" he called.

She felt the wool. "Yeah, but not too bad."

"Take a shirt, like I offered before. Second drawer in the dresser." He indicated the dark mahogany highboy.

"If you're sure." She walked back into the bedroom and opened the drawer. "Is this one okay?" She held up a plain white T-shirt. He nodded, and she slipped it over her head. She looked down. No, that would never do. She started to take the shirt off.

"No, don't," Jason said from the bed.

She looked over. "No? You don't think that it looks too slutty?" She looked at her chest again, reconfirming that her black bra was faintly visible through the white cotton.

"You've got something against slutty? Besides, did I ever tell you I have a thing for black underwear?"

Claire now looked to the ceiling. "I didn't choose the color to be provocative, if that's what you think. Over years of fieldwork and dubious washing conditions, I've found that black shows the least amount of wear and tear. It's strictly a utilitarian decision."

He crossed his arms, his biceps bulging very nicely, thank you. "That's what I like to hear. You realize that you've just demonstrated my—what is it now, sixth?— yes, sixth prerequisite for a future wife."

"What? A woman who doesn't do the wash very well?"

"No, a woman who can be practical and sexy at the same time. What do you think of that?"

Claire put her hands on her hips. "I have long since lost count of these ridiculous prerequisites, or whatever they are. Besides, I have it on good authority that you only have three requirements. Thirty-six, twenty-four, thirty-six."

"Those were my requirements when I was young and callow. Now I'm—"

"Older?"

"Never."

"Wiser?"

"Hardly."

"Then what's changed?"

He didn't answer.

She glanced at the mirror over the dresser, ran her fingers quickly through her hair, and sighed. "I'm sorry." She was. "As much as I'd like to keep up this banter all night, I really do have to go to work."

He dropped his arms to his side. "I'm coming with you."

"Don't be absurd. It's probably going to be a long night. And it's really boring, trust me."

"I'll bring a book." He bounded out of bed and walked briskly across the room to get some clothes out of the dresser, oblivious to his nakedness. Claire wasn't.

He grabbed another T-shirt from the drawer and pulled it on, found some boxers and slipped them on with a pair of well-worn jeans. He didn't bother with socks, but simply eased on a pair of loafers. He went to the desk in the living room and picked up a thick hardcover book.

Claire joined him. She turned her head sideways to read the title on the spine. *"Endocrinology and Responses to Hormonal Imbalances."* She looked puzzled. "A little light reading or do you use it to press flowers?"

Jason looked at the title himself. "Oh, it's just something Larry lent me. His idea of bedtime reading," he said, referring to his oncologist friend's taste in literature.

"Well, it could certainly put someone to sleep," Claire said. She stuffed her sweater in the top of her bag. Jason held open the door for her, and they went down to the lobby together.

Randolph looked long and hard as Jason handed over the key.

"He was staring at my chest," Claire whispered as they crossed the lobby.

"Would you rather he stared at my chest?" He placed his hand on the small of her back and steered her through the front door. He nodded to the doorman to hail a taxi.

"The magazine's only a ten-minute walk, you know."

"I know, but you'd be surprised the number of people who can recognize me in ten minutes. Anyway, it's chilly out and you don't have a coat."

Claire looked down and saw immediately that the cold air had instantly hardened her nipples. The black bra stood out with glaring obviousness.

Jason inclined his head toward her. "And there is that, as well, of course," he whispered as the doorman held open the door to the taxi.

By the time they arrived at *Focus*'s offices at around half past seven, the place was deserted. The deadline for putting the magazine to bed was still two days off, so the staff was taking advantage of a relatively normal work-day before the crunch set in.

They headed down the long hallway, decorated with scuffmarks and framed covers of back issues, and walked to the darkroom. It was the size of a closet. In fact, before it had had a fan and special lighting installed, it was a closet.

The door automatically shut behind them. Claire looked around. A half-emptied take-out coffee cup, left by another photographer, had been abandoned on the work counter. She reached over and dumped it in the garbage. Putting her camera bag on a stool, she emptied out roll after roll of film. She'd already carefully marked each with the date, place and subject with an indelible marker, so there wouldn't be any mix-ups after the fact. She lined them up methodically, then turned to Jason. "I'm just going to get some canisters and fix the developer. After that, I'll have to kill the lights, so it might be a little difficult for you to read." She looked around at the cramped quarters. Her bag was taking up the only seat. "Actually, it's pretty hard to read even with the light on. Maybe you want to wait outside at a desk?" She motioned to the door.

"So can you still see with the lights out?" he asked.

"Sure, you're working under a safe light then. Nothing will get ruined and people on the other side of the door know not to come in because an indicator goes on outside, as well." She flicked the switch and demonstrated.

Jason blinked at the warm, red glow. "I like it. It has that certain bordello appeal."

"Come off it. There's nothing sexy about the darkroom." She turned her back to him and poked around. "I hate it when other people move stuff. I can't find a thing."

"Wanna bet?" He came up behind her.

"That I can't find anything?" She arched her head up to look on the overhead shelves. The damn timer was nowhere in sight.

His hand came around, touching her chin. He gently turned her head sideways, then eased her body around to face him. "I meant about this place being sexy." He stepped closer, his hips and legs pressing into hers. The counter bit into her back. He kissed her lightly on the lips.

Claire paused. She tried to think of what she was going to say, and gave up when he kissed her again more deeply. "I see what you mean," she said when it was done.

He lifted her up, sitting her on the edge of the counter. Working a hand under the white shirt, he touched the bare skin at her waist. He pushed the shirt up to her breast. "This bra is just killing me." He rubbed his thumb across the swell of her breast through the lacy fabric. A moan escaped Claire's lips.

She wrapped her hands around his neck, entwining her fingers into his hair. "Well, I'm sure we can figure out how to put you out of your suffering."

11

CLAIRE UNLOCKED THE DOOR to Trish's apartment and quietly lowered her camera bag to the floor. It was only six o'clock in the morning. She was exhausted and high as a kite all at once. She desperately needed a shower, coffee and sleep. No, she was too wired for sleep.

She tiptoed across the living room rug, not wanting to make any noise that could wake Trish, not that she had ever been one to rise with the birds. Claire didn't feel up to giving a complete account of the night's activities. Ah, the night's activities. She smiled. In fact, a foolish grin seemed to have become affixed to her face, kind of like a deep-cleansing mud mask.

Unlike most shoeboxes in Manhattan that masquerade as apartments, Trish's place was fairly spacious—two bedrooms, with an L-shaped living room/dining room and a galley kitchen. Trish's parents had lived here when they first got married. At that time, these few blocks of the Upper East Side were considered a good "starter" neighborhood. When they moved to the suburbs with the birth of Trish's older sister and her father's promotions, they had shown remarkable forethought in not giving up the place. When it went co-op about twenty-five years ago, they bought it, and when Trish graduated from college, they gave it to her as a present. True, the white-brick building was ugly as sin, but a two-bedroom was a two-bedroom, especially with a doorman and an elevator.

Who knows what I could have come up with if I had stuck around to graduate, Claire mused as she gave a cursory glance to the mail that was piled on the coffee table. No, she'd been bored out of her gourd taking pictures of debating club presidents and visiting speakers for the campus newspaper, and she'd taken off at the end of junior year to see the world. A little too much of the world, it now seemed in retrospect. Whatever.

And besides, Big Jim had already joined the big photographer in the sky. And her mother? That simply wasn't part of the equation.

"Claire, is that you?"

Claire did a double take at the sound of Trish's voice. She peered around the living room to the adjoining dining area. The Bavarian crystal chandelier spilled light on the table. It was another of Trish's finds, this time from the Flea Market in Paris. The shipping bill had just about doubled the price. It gave the cleaning lady fits, since Trish insisted she clean it with some special vinegar solution she had read about in Hints from Heloise. The cleaning lady had a few hints of her own for Heloise.

Trish was seated at a chair at the end of the table. She wore a Natori silk peignoir, one spaghetti strap slipped artfully off-shoulder. Her hair tumbled around her neck, emphasizing its swanlike elegance. A pair of unlaced tennis shoes lay at her feet. A full-length mink coat was casually draped over the back of the chair.

"Back from a night on the town?" Claire asked, stopping next to the table. She saw the morning's papers spread out.

"I just couldn't wait to see if we got a mention in the tabloids, so I threw on a coat and rushed to the corner newsstand. Do you know how many people are up this time of day? It's appalling." Trish looked truly shocked.

"Speaking of which, you had a long session in the dark-room."

"Yeah, I'm still working on the assumption that it's night. I'm not ready to face daylight." There were a number of other things she wasn't prepared to face yet, either. She pointed to the paper that was opened to the gossip column. "So did you make the news?"

Trish slipped on her reading glasses and read, "'New York's newest sports star was seen squiring around a long-stemmed beauty yesterday, hitting such telling hot spots as the baby department of a local toy store and the ring counter of a major jewelry retail establishment. Been having more than breakfast with a certain someone, Jason Doyle?'"

Trish took off her glasses and looked at Claire. "I would have hoped that when they dished the dirt, they really named names, but the damage is done—so to speak."

"So to speak," Claire echoed.

Trish patted the place next to her at the table. "Have a seat. I need to tell you something."

"You do?"

Trish nodded anxiously.

Claire hooked her foot around the leg of a chair and dragged it away from the table. She sat down slowly. True confessions had a way of making her feel guilty.

"I think Jason could be the one."

Claire almost choked. "What?" She started coughing and Trish pounded her on the back.

"You all right there?"

Claire nodded, her eyes watery.

Trish folded her hands on top of the newspaper and leaned eagerly forward. "I said I think Jason could be the one."

"The one what?" Claire asked, afraid she already knew the answer.

"*The* one, silly. You know, Mr. Right."

"That's not good," Claire said quickly, maybe a little too frantically.

"No?"

"No."

"Why not?"

"Why not?" Yes, why not? "You said yourself that people don't just meet and have this lightning bolt of attraction suddenly strike them senseless."

"I'm feeling perfectly in control of my senses. What I'm experiencing isn't so much a lightning bolt as a warm feeling in my stomach."

"Trish, cocoa on a winter's day causes a warm feeling in your stomach. I don't think the desire to marry a man you've just met produces quite the same reaction."

Trish shifted on her seat. She didn't look the least bit convinced. "You've got to admit Jason's absolutely gorgeous."

Claire nodded reluctantly.

"Talented."

"Well, yes."

"Straight."

Claire had ample proof to verify that.

"Wealthy."

"You'd marry for money?" Claire was surprised.

"Not for money, but it is an attractive point. Added to which, he has a good sense of humor and can talk about a wide variety of subjects. What more can a girl with aging ovaries ask for?"

"Love?" Claire offered.

Trish chewed on her upper lip thoughtfully. "I'm thirty years old. The last time I thought I was in love, I was seventeen years old. How am I supposed to know what love feels like at my age? Besides, my expectations have mellowed since the days of slumber parties and shared peanut butter cups. Maybe a warm feeling in the stomach is love? Can you say it is or it isn't?"

Claire shook her head.

"I've got to go with my instincts. And my instincts tell me Jason is a terrific guy. If he isn't Mr. Right at this stage, he's Mr. Almost Right. After this weekend, who knows?" She reached across the table and patted Claire's hand. "And I owe it all to you."

Claire smiled feebly. She didn't have the heart to tell her best friend that she had just spent the past twelve hours or so making love to the man of her dreams. She simply couldn't blurt, "You can't have him because I think I may feel something for him that goes beyond lust, may actually be the start of love, but because I'm too much of an emotional coward to dissect my feelings, and because I'm afraid of how vulnerable I might become if I were to feel for someone that much, I may never know for sure." Or something more coherent to that effect. How could she confess these thoughts to the only person who'd ever given her unqualified friendship and support? How could she?

She couldn't.

Claire slipped her hand out of Trish's and pushed back the chair. "I wouldn't give me that much credit." She hesitated. Did she have the nerve to say something after all? "I do have one thing to say though."

"Yes?" Trish was all ears.

Claire looked at her scrubbed face, devoid of makeup. Her artless hairstyle—there was even a piece of hair sticking out at an odd angle next to her ear. Trish almost looked seventeen again, with a certain innocence that

Claire hadn't seen in a long time. Could she wipe that away with a few words? "You know, I wouldn't call you an arbiter of fashion sense this early in the morning." She kicked at a sneaker as she walked to the kitchen. "Why don't I make some coffee and get you back into high fashion gear?"

The answer was she didn't.

CLAIRE DIDN'T BOTHER TO RUSH to the ceremony at the Waldorf that evening. Not that the ornate luxury hotel on the Upper East Side wasn't acceptable—they did have the best women's bathrooms, bar none. No, it's just that she knew the first hour would be taken up with cocktails and endless chatter, followed by a three-course meal consisting of some smoked salmon salad, veal medallions and chocolate soufflé. Rubber chicken was just not done anymore. Then would come an introductory speech that would last as long as the complete Ring Cycle, and finally the awards presentation.

She had thought about calling Jason during the day. More than once she had thought about calling him. Both of them had been too tied up to get together. He with team meetings, working out, contract talks with Vernon, including a house contract; she with finishing developing her film, printing shots for Trish to take to the wedding, and marking some possible shots for the story—she still needed to see a rough-out of Trish's copy before making her final recommendations. She was also scheduled to try out one of the new digital cameras that *Focus* had ordered. There were definite advantages to these high-tech puppies, but her trusty Leica had a familiar weight and feel. Claire wasn't a Luddite when it came to technology. She enjoyed tinkering with the latest electronic gadgets. But at this stage in her life, she liked to keep things simple, familiar. And she also couldn't help thinking that relegating her Leica to the shelf would be like abandoning her father's only legacy.

If it were only her father on her mind at the moment, Claire could probably deal with it. But for the first time in his life and afterlife, Big Jim was eclipsed by another man. When she pictured a face, she saw Jason's, laughing as they tumbled to the floor of the darkroom. If she heard a voice, it was Jason's teasing her about her hair, calling out her name during sex. If she conjured up a scent, it was the smell of Jason's skin right behind his ear—indefinably masculine and sweet at the same time.

How someone had come to consume her thoughts, her senses, in such a short time was a mystery. She should feel overwhelmed. Instead she felt empowered. She should feel imprisoned. Instead she felt liberated.

And then there was Trish. She really did need to talk to Jason, as much as the idea of the conversation frightened her to death. But this type of conversation was not something you had on a cell phone while riding the Lexington Avenue subway with fellow straphangers close enough to hear all the gory details. Or so she told herself.

Claire looked at her watch. Eight-thirty—p.m. They'd probably just finished coffee. She flashed her press pass and invitation at the ballroom door and slipped into the back of the large room. Other photographers lined the walls. She nodded to the ones she knew. All around, tables were filled with politicians, sports figures and writers, successful business types, overwhelmingly male— black and white—with young, well-manicured, high-maintenance dates basking in the collective limelight. Diamonds sparkled from their ears, necks and hands—the limelight was radiating overtime.

She immediately spotted Jason up on the dais. Never

had a man done so much for a charcoal-gray suit. Let's face it, she admitted, the man could do wonders for sackcloth and ashes. To his left sat Vernon, his hair gel gleaming. To Jason's right—Trish clad in a silvery slip dress and a prominent collarbone. *Mirabile dictu*, both skinny straps were still in place. Oops, no, she'd spoken too soon. As Trish bent her head and smiled at something Jason was saying to her, a wayward strap headed downward. She looked very sexy, glittery happy.

Claire felt a lump the size and heft of a Butterball turkey—still frozen, with giblets inside—forming in her stomach. She was going to have to say something, do something, before her friend got hurt. Just what, she was still unsure of.

She glanced at the rest of the table on the raised platform and was surprised to recognize a few other faces. Larry—Dr. Lawrence Shepherd—from the hospital they visited the other day, was there. She knew the award was to recognize the charitable contributions made by Jason's foundation, so maybe she should have guessed the connection. But she never would have predicted that Jason's friend Simone Fahrer would be present, as well. Next to her was this bruiser of a fellow—a big, blond, rugged lumberjack type. From the way she picked a thread off his jacket sleeve—a true female, proprietary marking—he had to be her husband, Ted Daniger. Claire saw him tip back his chair and exchange some remarks with Jason. Yes, they were definitely buddies. How they fitted into the awards business was still unexplained.

Claire felt a tingle run down her neck. She looked back at Jason and saw that he had spotted her. He lifted his chin and smiled. The corner of her mouth lifted in pleased acknowledgment. Nervously, she looked down and fiddled with her camera.

She listened as the introductory speaker, who Claire recognized as the television broadcaster Amos Greig—known for his aphorisms and his pompadour-style toupee—moved from the obligatory jokes to the business at hand. "Now, it's my pleasure and privilege on behalf of the Professional Athletes Association to honor this young man, Jason Doyle, from the north country of Vermont for distinguished community service. I'm sure his mother would be very proud of him today."

Jason nodded modestly.

"Jason, as you all know, is founder and president of the Daniel Daniger Fund."

No, she didn't know. Daniel Daniger Fund? Was that some relation to Ted Daniger?

"The Daniger Fund has played a major role in supporting cancer research over the years, and here to give a personal perspective on its contribution is Dr. Lawrence Shepherd, Chief of Oncology at Frankston Memorial Hospital, here in our own fair city. Dr. Shepherd?"

Larry took his turn at the podium. He unfolded a speech, but instead of reading off his script, he looked directly at Jason. "Jason, you and I go back a long way, maybe too long," he said.

"Speak for yourself, Larry," Jason quipped.

"What I can say," Larry went on, "is that it's been a journey, full of bumps, some of them exciting, some of them frustrating, and some of them sad." Claire saw Simone Fahrer grasp Ted Daniger's hand.

"When we first met eleven years ago, I had more hair and you were just generating attention as a college hockey player with a lethal slap shot and a short fuse for a temper. Didn't you lead the NCAAs that year in scoring as well as penalties?" Larry asked. Jason acknowledged with an embarrassed shake of the head. The crowd laughed. "But probably what set your temper off the most was what you considered to be your helplessness at stopping a disease that was inextricably taking the life of your roommate and best friend, Danny Daniger."

Jason reached for a water glass and sipped thoughtfully.

"I remember when things got close to the end, your frustration would boil over into anger at me, and I seriously wondered if one of those hard hits you were known for on the ice was going to come my way. The day that Danny died, you hunted me down, found me in the doctors' lounge. Everybody else knew enough to clear out, but I knew there was no point in running because I had been the only person known to crawl the hundred-meter sprint in seventh grade phys ed—and that had been the height of my athletic prowess." Some nervous snickers penetrated the hushed gathering.

"So I steeled myself for a heavy blow, figuring that if you hit my face, the damage might actually render an improvement. I must confess, despite my steely determination to be brave, I took a step back. You stepped forward." The snickers disappeared. "And then you said to me in a very low voice, 'You did everything you could, but it wasn't enough.' I think I nodded, still unsure what would happen next. And then you raised your arm and I'm pretty sure I flinched. But instead of decking me, you placed your hand on my shoulder and you said, 'We're going to have to do something to give you more to work with.'"

Larry stopped and wiped his mouth.

Claire gulped. Her throat was tight.

"And that's when the Daniel Daniger Fund for Cancer Research was born. We still don't have everything we need to wipe out the disease, but you and the fund have given us—given me—more. And for that I want to thank you as a doctor and as a friend. Jason, it's been a wonderful eleven years." Larry gathered his papers, stopped at Jason's side, and shook hands.

Claire pointed and shot the picture. Click.

Amos knew his cue. He returned to the podium. "Jason Doyle, come up and accept this award that you so richly deserve." Jason stood, buttoning his suit jacket.

Claire readied her camera for the money shot. Amos needed two hands to lift the massive Lalique glass trophy. It vaguely resembled a New Age Winged Victory. Jason liberated it from Amos's shaky hands.

Click.

Smiled and shook hands.

Click.

Then he carefully lowered the trophy to the table, and turned to address the crowd. Everyone was standing and clapping.

"Thank you, Larry, for your moving words. And thank you, Amos—actually, this may be the first time I've thanked a reporter." Amos answered with a salute. "Most importantly, let me extend my thanks to the Professional Athletes Association for recognizing the work of the Daniel Daniger Fund. As I've always said, the force behind the fund was and will always be Danny. I just came along for the ride. There are many worthy causes out there, and many people contribute far more than me. I'm lucky enough to work with inspired and inspiring people who make my efforts that much more rewarding. And speaking of rewards, I expect to see all of you—" he pointed around the room "—out there at the annual Daniel Daniger Fund celebrity golf tournament next spring. Thank you again." Jason waved his hand, touching the trophy at the same time.

Click.

The applause was deafening. Amos hugged him.

Click.

Larry came over.

Click.

Simone gave him a kiss; Ted, a telling handshake.

Click.

And when it was over, Claire lowered her camera. And wiped her eyes.

And then she knew. She loved him.

SHE WAITED IN THE FOYER for Jason to come out. The crowd was gradually thinning. Most of the reporters had finished their questions. The women had liberated their furs from the coat check. Finally, Jason came out with Vernon and Trish. Vernon was on his cell phone. Trish was hanging on Jason's arm. She waved when she saw Claire, and dragged him over.

"Wasn't he amazing? Gorgeous, generous and humble." She beamed a smile at Jason and looked to Claire for confirmation of what she already knew to be true.

"The answer to every girl's dreams," Claire responded in the expected glib fashion.

"Especially when coupled with an outstanding endorsement package that's just about sewn up," Vernon said, coming up next to them.

"And I owe it all to mom and apple pie," Jason deadpanned. He turned to Vernon and Trish. "I just need to talk to Claire a sec. I'll catch up with you in a minute."

"We'll wait for you in the front lobby," Vernon said, and he helped Trish on with her vintage Persian lamb jacket.

Jason watched them move on, chatting away. He turned his attention back to Claire. "I see you dressed for the occasion," he said jokingly, tugging at her lock of gray hair.

Claire blushed and surveyed her clothes—black jeans, black turtleneck and a black fleece vest. "At least it's basic black. I'm sorry. I rushed over from the darkroom. I was running behind because someone distracted me from working last night."

Jason smiled the same goofy grin that Claire had walked around with most of the day. "Yeah, I seem to remember something along those lines."

"Funny about that." They stood there grinning at each other.

"It was fun, wasn't it?" Jason ran a hand lightly up and down her sleeve. "I was hoping you could come over later tonight, but Vernon's stopping by to talk about the last details of the endorsement deal, and that may run pretty late."

"Don't worry. I'm really bushed anyway. There'll be other nights."

He reached down for her hand and laced his fingers through hers. "There will be other nights, won't there?"

Claire tilted her head, enjoying the warmth of his hand. "Jason, we have to talk."

"I know." He brought their linked hands to his mouth and kissed the back of hers. "I wish this whole wedding farce were over and we could see each other without tiptoeing around."

Claire liked the way he said tiptoeing. "What about tomorrow morning?"

Jason shook his head. "I can't make it tomorrow morning. I've got to drive down to Grantham to talk to some contractors about the house." His eyes lighted up. "I've rented a Porsche. Wanna come?"

"I can't. I have a meeting at the office to start setting up another assignment. Can't you have Vernon handle the contractors instead?"

"I could, but I don't want him to. It's my house. I'm the one who's going to live there." His voice was firm.

Claire nodded. "I understand."

"What about in the afternoon?"

"No, I still can't make it. I have to take the train up early to Leeds Springs to discuss the details of the wedding pictures. When are you coming?"

"Tomorrow evening—in time for the rehearsal dinner. I'm driving Trish."

Claire frowned. "That's right." She looked imploringly into his eyes. "How can it be this difficult for two people to see each other alone?"

A woman's voice interrupted them.

"Trouble in paradise?" Simone asked as she and Ted spied them after they'd walked out of the ballroom.

Claire and Jason immediately broke apart. They seemed to do a lot of that whenever Simone was around.

"Hi, Simone, good to see you again," Claire said, mustering an air of calm that she certainly wasn't feeling. She offered her hand to Ted. "I'm Claire Marsden."

Simone turned to her husband. "She's going to tell you she's just the photographer."

"Oh, so she's the one." Ted gave her a firm handshake. "Simone has told me all about you."

I just bet, Claire thought.

"Ted and Simone both sit on the board of the foundation," Jason explained.

"The foundation seems to be doing wonderful work," Claire said, quickly picking up on the change of topic. "I hadn't heard a lot about it, and I was interested to hear that you support not only research into a cure but promote new forms of palliative care."

Simone looked approvingly to Ted. "See, I told you she wasn't one of his usual bimbos."

"Excuse me," Jason sounded mildly offended. "I never considered any of my bimbos 'usual.'"

Simone leaned toward Claire and spoke sotto voce but distinctly enough for someone's grandmother in Great Neck to hear. "Listen, do us all a favor, especially Jason. Tell him to grow up and get his act together. Finish, damn it." She gave Jason the evil eye, then turned back to Claire. "He won't listen to me, and God knows I've tried. But I have a feeling he'd listen to you."

Claire was mystified. "Finish what?"

"Simone, give the guy a break." The strong arm of Ted Daniger came to rest lightly on her shoulder.

"I only bug him because I know." She searched Jason's face. "You're on the top of your game now, but what happens when you blow out your knee or get your umpteenth concussion? You going to open some steakhouse or do commentary on a cable sports channel?"

"Maybe I could do commentary from the steakhouse?" Jason suggested jokingly.

"Jason, will you grow up?" Simone pleaded.

"Why should I when I'm having so much fun?" he answered.

"Argh." Simone held up her arms in disgust.

Ted kneaded her shoulder. "He knows, sweetheart. He's just teasing you."

Trish wandered back to the hallway, signaling them to hurry up.

Simone sighed. "Sometimes I'm not so sure. I mean, I'm sure he knows, but there's knowing and then there's doing something about it." She turned a stern eye on Claire. "So I'm counting on you to help him see the light. And don't tell me you're just the photographer."

12

SHE SURE HAD GREAT TEETH.

Natalie Goad was a great advertisement for her own product. If Claire ever had a preadolescent with an overbite, Natalie would definitely be her first choice in orthodontic care.

In fact, there were a lot of admirable qualities about Natalie Goad. She stood up when she introduced herself. She wore really cool glasses—the kind that some French jazz musician from the fifties might have worn. And she harbored a misguided fantasy that the Baltimore Orioles were actually going to win the World Series.

Only problem was, she was marrying David Bruckner—Trish's David—and Claire felt like a traitor if she allowed herself to like Natalie.

"I'm so glad you and Patti could come to the wedding. David has talked a lot about you two, and I've always wanted to meet you," Natalie said over coffee.

"You have?" Claire reached for the creamer. They were seated in the glass-enclosed sunroom of a historical hotel located on a back road east of Leeds Springs. The kind of back road that twisted and turned and was lined with low stone walls decorating hobby farms for the rich and idle.

The "chosen" wedding guests and the bridal party itself got to stay at the hotel, one of those pre-Revolutionary War inns that had survived the British invasion but ultimately succumbed to an onslaught of Laura Ashley. As was typical of these cozily exorbitant places, it had a jocular animal name, in this case, the Dancing Frog Inn. The little green fellow did a jig on the complimentary matchbooks and cream-colored stationery. The gift shop also sold homemade jams and relishes, tea towels, pot holders and one-hundred-percent silk ties emblazoned with dancing frogs. Practically the only things they didn't sell with dancing frogs were frog legs, which would have seemed to be highly appropriate in a dismembered sort of way.

"You really have wanted to meet us?" Claire asked again.

"Of course." Natalie nodded enthusiastically. "I believe that we are a sum total of all our experiences, and having only met David at this point in life, it helps me to put him in context if I meet some of his childhood friends. Don't you agree?"

"Well, I guess so. I still think it's pretty brave of you. I'm not sure I could face down some people from my earlier life. Like Mrs. Hornung, our twelfth-grade American history teacher. The thought of her frightens me even now."

"That bad?"

"Trust me, that bad. No one else got the janitor to wash her blackboards each day but Mrs. Hornung. I'm not sure if it was blackmail or what."

Natalie listened intently. "I must remember to double-check the guest list to see if David invited her for nostalgia's sake."

"I think you might be safe. Mrs. Hornung is probably terrorizing the Great Janitor in the sky by now."

Natalie chuckled. "That's comforting." She sipped her coffee and slowly lowered her china cup. "I suppose it's time for us to talk about what I really need to talk to you about."

"Right, the photos." Claire pulled out a notebook and ballpoint pen from her camera bag. "I presume you want mostly color, with maybe one roll of black-and-white, a mixture of formal and so-called 'journalistic' shots. If there are certain people or groupings you want to be sure I get, you should tell me now. I find as much communication up front is beneficial for everyone, and then you won't feel you've missed out on anything afterward." Claire looked up and waited for Natalie to give her the word.

There was a silence.

Claire clicked her pen. "We could start with the immediate family members."

Natalie stared at her coffee cup, holding the delicate handle in her fingers. "I do want to talk to you about the wedding photos, and I really appreciate all you're doing. It's very generous, and especially exciting to think that Claire Marsden is taking the pictures. But..." She looked into the depths of her coffee cup again. "Help," she called out softly, sloshing the last bits around the inside of the porcelain.

This did not look good. Claire had heard of pre-wedding jitters, and she was definitely getting the feeling that Natalie was not as confident as she had first appeared. Claire leaned forward and said quietly, "I don't think freshly brewed coffee has quite the prognostic powers of tea leaves. Not that I'm an expert, but I'm pretty sure that if it did, some coffeehouse would already be exploiting it in some way." She paused, still no response. "Is there something you wanted to tell me? I have absolutely no experience when it comes to marital bliss, but I'm very good at nodding at the right moments."

Natalie pursed her lips. She looked across the table. "I lied. I'm not wildly enthusiastic about having you and Patti here. No, that's not right. I'm fine about you being here—"

"Thanks, I think," Claire said.

Natalie smiled a nervous smile. "It's Patti—sorry, it's Trish now, right?"

Claire nodded.

"I know it's probably foolish, but I have this gut feeling that in some fundamental way, David is still in love with her. I guess it's the lasting power of first loves and all that. I wouldn't know, because I spent more time in biology lab in high school than going out with boys," Natalie confessed.

"I know what you mean," Claire said.

"Anyhow, David wanted you both to come, and I pretended I was all happy about the whole thing. But deep down, I'm jealous. I'm even scared that David will see her and decide an orthodontist with glasses simply doesn't live up to his high school memories."

"But your glasses are really cool. I was just thinking they're one of your best features."

"You think?" Natalie smiled, and when she did, she really was pretty, Claire thought. "Anyway—" she shrugged her shoulders "—there's this part of me that's scared sick about what may happen this weekend. And then there's this other part of me that says, 'Hey, you're committing yourself to this man who you love, truly love, but if there is some doubt about the whole thing, better to find out now. Let my husband-to-be realize that the real thing—me—is better than the fantasy—Patti, alias Trish. And if he doesn't realize that...'" Her voice trailed off. She looked up beseechingly. "Do you think I'm right to be concerned? Or do you think I'm worrying over nothing?"

Claire opened her mouth and closed it. Should she tell Natalie she was right to have doubts? That Trish, too, was agonizing about David, old love and new love? That she herself was wondering desperately whether she should tell Trish that she was also pondering the possibility of true love with a man, who by every indication was terrific but who, at the moment, not only led a totally different lifestyle than she, complete with glitter and fame and whose feelings she wasn't really sure about except that he appeared to lust for her body exceptionally nicely—was that love?—but who was also currently tied up pretending to be Trish's new true love?

She could barely think the thoughts straight, let alone voice them to a woman, who by all indications seemed very nice and perfectly suited to life in Chicago with a district attorney.

So Claire opened her mouth and said with all the confidence she wasn't feeling, "Take it from me. It's best to get these things out in the open. It's when people start tiptoeing around—" she decided she loved that expression "—that problems occur."

She didn't know how prescient those words were— even without tea leaves.

As seemed to be the fashion these days, the rehearsal dinner was more of a night-before-the-big-event dinner. Anybody who was in town the night before showed up for Cornish hens stuffed with wild rice and a medley of fall vegetables. The chef at the Dancing Frog appeared to aspire to "colonial cuisine goes vertical"—the winter squash and beet combo was stacked like a Lower East

Side Reuben sandwich and the Cornish hen sat on its haunches, looking vaguely obscene.

It was all going pretty well—if one ignored the provocative pose of the bird—even though the bride-to-be was drinking a little too much and the groom-to-be was repeatedly called away on the telephone to deal with a racketeering trial currently in the jury-selection stage. Vernon had arrived halfway into cocktails and was surprisingly charming and low-key. He had turned off his phone, brought Natalie's mother five pounds of Belgian chocolate for being so accommodating at the last minute, and bought at least forty dollars' worth of Dancing Frog tchotchkes for his daughter. He also seemed perfectly capable of amusing himself while Claire was tied up taking candid photos of family members and friends.

Many of the people, at least those on David's side of the family, she knew from years ago. She hadn't seen his father in more than ten years, but he gave her a big hug and told her she had to come jogging with him in the morning.

"I thought your idea of morning exercise was running to catch the six forty-five to New York," she said.

"That was before my angioplasty." Mr. Bruckner tapped his heart. "It was a real wake-up call. Don't let stress ruin your life. Enjoy yourself."

"I'm trying to," Claire said. And the thing of it was, she really was. "Maybe you should tell that to Dave, though." She indicated his son who was holed up next to a brass wall sconce, talking rapidly on the phone.

"You're absolutely right. Take care, dear. It's good to see you again. I always thought you were going places." Mr. Bruckner gave her another hug—as much from the heart, expansive and now healthy, as from some newly toned biceps.

"Claire, dear, isn't it nice that they treat you as one of the guests."

Claire didn't need to turn around to recognize her mother's voice. And she was seriously contemplating not bothering to at all, but at this mature stage in her life, she decided that would be childish. She would just have to save her bad behavior for later.

So she did the right thing and, turning around, said with a smile, "Mother, but I am one of the guests."

"Well, you know what I mean." Claire's mother raised one eyebrow and scrutinized her daughter. For once, Claire wasn't wearing jeans or the equivalent. She had splurged on a line of knitwear that was mix-and-match, based around simply cut black dresses or slacks. The clothes were definitely more formfitting than Claire was used to, but she was delighted that her hips actually looked good and you couldn't see the line of her underpants. Besides, they were machine washable, thus justifying the outrageous price. Just think of the dry cleaning bills she was saving on. Tonight she wore the scooped neck, calf-length dress.

"That's a stunning dress," her mother remarked.

Claire was shocked. Her mother was giving her a compliment. "Thank you, Mother. You're looking well." Her helmet hair silhouetted her high cheekbones. Emerald-and-diamond earrings were clipped into her earlobes with the ferocity of Doberman pinschers. Despite years of exposure to the sun on the golf links, her mother's skin was surprisingly elastic. Don't be naive, Claire chided herself. It's not surprising at all.

"But you really should wear a strong lipstick color with black," her mother added.

Claire rolled her eyes. She should have known. "I'll remember that next time."

"I have a tube of red—very good, Elizabeth Arden—in my purse." She started to fumble through her beaded handbag.

"Don't worry. It's not necessary."

"Nonsense. I have it right here. You can just touch up in the powder room." She handed over the silver tube. She had laid down the gauntlet.

Claire hesitated, then took the lipstick. "I'll put it on when I get the chance."

Her mother sighed. "You haven't changed, have you?"

What could she say that wouldn't sound confrontational and still contain a spark of truth? Far better to change the subject. "So is William here with you?" Claire asked about her stepfather.

"No, the poor man has a board meeting in the city for the St. Andrew's Society." Claire's stepfather took his Scottish roots on his mother's side extremely seriously. But then, how many other babies born in Flint, Michigan in 1943 had been christened William Wallace Quinn? "He promised he'd be here for the wedding tomorrow, however, even though large public gatherings that don't involve shareholders are not his cup of tea," her mother explained.

Not his shot of whiskey was probably more like it. Still, Claire was saved from further comment by the sound of gravel crunching on the circular drive in front of the inn.

"I wonder who's arriving this late?" Claire's mother asked, turning her head to get a view through the window. Even though it was dark, the lanterns out front tastefully lit up the entrance. "Look, dear, isn't that Patricia?" She walked closer to the window and peered out between the layers of Belgian lace and green swags.

Claire joined her. She squinted and saw a black—at least, it looked black in the dark—Porsche parked out front. Trish had opened the passenger side door and extended a long leg. Long was an understatement. It stretched about the length of U.S. 1 from Maine to Florida. On her foot was a skimpy little sandal with a stiletto heel. It warranted its expensive price tag not so much for what it was made of but for what it implied. At the top of her thigh—somewhere—seemed to be the edge of a dress.

Trish stood. Again it was definitely a matter of implication. Claire had thought her own dress was a bit body-hugging. Trish's snappy little number made a toothpaste tube look like a loose burlap bag. At least the long sleeves stayed put on her shoulders. Then she turned. Claire gasped. Trish's dress was backless. And waistless, as well. With a bit of extended movement, it could also become buttockless.

"Oh, my," said Claire's mother. "That girl always did like to create attention." She peered more closely. "I see she has on matching lipstick."

Leave it to her mother to insult her even when she was talking about someone else.

"My, my, and who is that handsome young man she's with?" Her mother held away the edge of the curtain with a well-manicured hand.

Claire looked over her shoulder. "That's Trish's fiancé," she said casually. She found it difficult to say the words.

"Fiancé? I didn't know she was engaged. There wasn't any announcement in the *New York Times*." Her mother craned her neck to get an even better view. Jason unknowingly obliged her as he opened the trunk and reached in to retrieve a garment bag and a suitcase. He bent over again and lifted up a suit jacket. Facing them, he shrugged it on. He straightened the cuffs and collar of his dress shirt and ran a hand quickly through his hair.

"My, my, indeed." Claire's mother brought her hand up to the corner of her mouth. Was that a little bit of dribble that Claire spotted? "Do you know who he is? He looks somewhat familiar."

Claire breathed in deeply. "Jason Doyle."

Claire's mother turned and frowned. "Isn't he some kind of sports star?"

"Hockey player," Claire answered with a practiced monotone.

Her mother sniffed. "Patricia and a hockey player? I never would have pictured that." She paused. "More someone you would bring home."

"Me?" Claire was incredulous.

"Don't look so incredulous, dear. After all, you were the one who loved to gallivant around the world with your father, chasing after rhinos and climbing mountains."

"Still, a hockey star?" Claire knew she was fishing for something, but she wasn't sure what she wanted to hear from her mother. Yes, from her mother of all people.

"What do you mean 'still'? You shouldn't underestimate your attractiveness, Claire." She went back to staring out the window. "Even if you could improve your appearance by wearing lipstick. There seems to be something in the back seat. Can you make it out?"

Claire peered more closely. Jason opened the driver's side door again and pushed the back of his seat forward. Holding the door partly closed, he pulled out another soft-sided bag, placed that on the ground, leaned over, giving a very nice view of his rear end and thighs—Claire heard her mother's sharp intake of breath—and slipped out a small duffel bag. Then he bent once more to get something else. It was like the stateroom scene from a Marx Brothers movie, only in reverse. Trish came around that side, as well.

"What is it they've got in there?" Claire's mother asked.

Whatever it was, it appeared to be large. And it appeared to be moving. And it wasn't in there anymore. In the car, that is. It was on the driveway. On a leash.

"My God, is that a bear?" Claire's mother asked.

Trish backed out of the way hurriedly—an extraordinary feat, considering the construction of her shoes. "No, it's not a bear," Claire said. "It's a dog. A very large dog." An enormous bow flopped from its collar as it nervously stretched the leash in the direction of a tree.

"It's an Akita," her mother said.

Claire saw it lift its leg on a branch. "No, I think it's a holly."

Her mother turned to her. "I know the tree is a holly. We have two flanking the drive on either side of the house. We put little white lights on them every Christmas."

Claire frowned. "You do? I don't remember that."

Her mother waved her off impatiently. "I started doing it after you moved out. But I'm not talking about the tree. I'm talking about the dog. It's an Akita."

Claire's eyes widened, and she watched as Jason juggled the bags and the dog up the stairway. "So that's an Akita."

"I wonder what it's doing here. Patricia has a dog?" She pulled back from the window when Trish and Jason went through the front door and out of view.

"She didn't as of this morning." And then Claire had this sinking feeling. "Oh, no." She clutched her camera nervously.

A few minutes later, Jason and Trish swept into the room. All eyes turned. Conversation stopped. All that was missing was a spotlight and maybe two groups of chorus girls, coming out of the wings in feathers—the girls, that is, not the wings, at least not those kind of wings.

But props were unnecessary. Sometimes less is more.

Even the dog was nowhere to be seen.

They made a spectacular couple. Jason, with his dark hair and dark suit, the embodiment of rugged masculinity barely harnessed in fine tailoring. Trish, her willowy frame wrapped in her itty-bitty red dress, a delicate counterpoint to his granite strength.

They held hands. Jason seemed only to have eyes for her. Claire felt a reflexive punch to the gut. He murmured something. She laughed lyrically. Their joined hands swung playfully.

Trish's eyes sparkled with anticipation. And, Claire realized, at this moment they were only on David, who was approaching from across the room. That should make her feel better. But it didn't.

It looked as if he had left Natalie in a lurch without a thought. She was stuck watching him rush off and having to talk with—oh, no, it couldn't be, yes, it was—Mrs. Hornung, their twelfth grade American history teacher. No wonder Natalie took a large gulp of champagne.

"David," Trish called, doing her best imitation of Bette Davis in *All About Eve*. All she needed was a cigarette holder. No, she didn't need the cigarette holder. Less is more.

David made a beeline for her. What did Trish see when she watched the frantic approach of her youthful lover? Did she still see a skinny boy with brown hair, a quick wit, and the slowest time for the high hurdles on the track team?

Claire remembered him for skeptically accepting her, as much because he respected her talent as because he wanted to get laid by her best friend.

Now when she looked over at David, she saw a successful-looking man in his early thirties with slightly thinning brown hair, who took himself a little too seriously, but not seriously enough that he wouldn't admit to his abysmal performance on a cinder track years earlier. Harvard admissions hadn't cared, either, Claire recalled.

"Jason Doyle. I can't tell you what a pleasure it is to meet you." David's cell phone was nowhere in view for the first time all evening. "I've been a fan of yours for so, so long," he gushed, holding out his hand excitedly.

Jason calmly shook it. "I hope not all that long." He smiled.

David laughed nervously. "I was really hoping you'd come to Chicago. We could desperately use some of your offensive ability." Jason looked down. David looked down. And realized that he was still pumping Jason's hand. "Oh, sorry." He dropped it like a hot potato. And for the first time, he seemed to notice the other member of the little group. "Patti, it's great to see you." He leaned to kiss her cheek.

Trish stepped forward, her arms outstretched for a full hug. David awkwardly placed his hands on her back, flesh touching flesh. He pulled back haltingly, took in her face—Trish favored him with a full-wattage smile of beautiful teeth that even Natalie would admire if it weren't for the fact that they belonged to Patti alias Trish. "It's great to have the old high school gang together

again. And to think, you're here with Jason Doyle, Patti,"
he said.

This was worse than Claire could ever have predicted.
And she was pretty good at foreseeing gloom and doom.
She had pictured David running off with Trish after one
look. Or Natalie, so upset with being jilted, that she
blindly drove down the wrong side of the Hutchinson
River Parkway. Or Trish, after deciding that David's hair
was too thin for her liking, bundling Jason into the Porsche and taking off for points unknown that nonetheless
took VISA.

She had never imagined David thinking Trish was part
of the "old gang."

She looked at Trish. She looked stunned. A deer caught
in the headlights was a cliché, but it was apt. Bambi finding out about his mother's death was even more on the
mark. Claire knew she had to act. She quickly walked
over.

Jason, sensitive lad that he was, had already picked up
on the tension. "Patti? Oh, that's right, Trish's name from
her childhood." He put an arm around Trish's shoulder
and squeezed it. "I was so happy when she asked me to
join her this weekend. You really find out so much more
about the person you love when you meet people from
their past."

"Don't you?" Natalie joined the group—with champagne glass in hand. "Patti? It is Patti, isn't it?" Natalie
extended her hand à la Auntie Mame. It was the battle of
old Hollywood stars. "And Jason, what an honor to have
you here at our little gathering." She fluttered her fingers
in his direction, as well, and took a sip of champagne.
Even he looked stunned.

Claire jumped into the fray. "Oh, guys, isn't this great.

Everybody together. Let me get a shot while the night is still young."

"Although, apparently not young enough. I don't think we've met." Claire's mother stepped forward. She held out her hand to Jason, signaling Claire at the same time with her eyebrows.

"Mother, Jason Doyle. Jason, this is my mother, Sheila Quinn."

Jason smiled politely. "Quinn?"

"Yes, I remarried after Claire's late father," she said. What she didn't say was that Claire's father was still firmly above ground when her second marriage had taken place. The ink was hardly dry on her divorce papers—Claire was four at the time—before she'd made her marriage to the senior vice president of an insurance underwriters firm, in charge of agricultural enterprises, official. Claire's stepfather knew more about John Deere tractors than any man with a three-acre lot in suburbia and a full-time grounds service. They were also something of a macho overcompensation for a fear of dogs. The ceremony was brief and the bride wore a cream silk shantung suit with a discreet pearl brooch on the lapel. Claire received a five-by-seven copy of the official photo nine months later.

"You don't seem old enough to be Claire's mother." Vernon's dulcet tones cut through the emotional miasma. "I'm Vernon Ehrenreich, Claire's date for the wedding." He studied her mother. "On second thought, there is a definite family resemblance—those high cheekbones. They put a Russian czarina's to shame." Claire saw her mother blush. "And, Jason, good to see you, buddy." He gave Jason's stiff figure a hug. "Trish, what can I say? Spectacular dress." He kissed her frozen cheek. A little color returned.

Never would Claire have said that an agent would be the one to save the day, but at that moment, Vernon was a deserving candidate for the Croix de Guerre, or at the very least, an Academy Award. Tonight, he was earning every penny of his fifteen percent.

"Maybe we could round up some glasses for a toast?" Claire flagged down a waiter.

"I could use a top-up." Natalie held out her glass.

"Could I get a picture of just Jason and me, too?" David asked sheepishly. "I'm just such a fan, you see. The fellows at the office won't believe it."

"Maybe Claire can make me a print, as well? It's not every day I get to stand next to a district attorney. I don't usually travel in such lofty circles." Jason slapped him on the back. Soundly. David seemed to enjoy the pain.

"Perhaps I should step to the side and let the youngsters be in the picture?" Claire's mother suggested modestly.

Claire sighed. She knew she was supposed to beg her mother to step back in.

"Nonsense, three glamorous women in one photo can only be better than two." Vernon could shovel with the best of them.

Claire readied her camera. "Don't look at me. Talk among yourselves. Cuddle up closer." All the women took this to mean they could latch on to Jason. Not surprisingly, Claire's mother got the biggest piece. "Now, let's all raise those glasses. Clink them together carefully. We don't want to spill any of that bubbly."

Trish, who had been moving in a semicatatonic state, seemed to suddenly snap out of it. "Hold everything, Claire. Stop the cameras." Trish held up her hands dramatically. "I have something special for the two lovebirds," she gushed. "And it'll be perfect for the photo."

Oh, no. Claire had a sinking feeling.

"Just a minute, I have to get it from the front desk." Trish turned, displaying a remarkable amount of taut back cleavage and a pair of well-toned thighs and calves. For a woman whose idea of working out was taking a taxi to Barney's for end-of-season sales, Trish looked supremely fit.

Within seconds Trish returned. Or rather she was pulled by what appeared to be an enormous golden bow. Attached to a large furry dog. "Natalie and David, this is for you." She held out the leash. The dog's tail quivered nervously at the sight of all the people.

Claire stepped forward. "Trish, maybe now isn't the best time."

Natalie turned to David. "Is it a circus bear?"

David frowned. "No, I think a circus bear would have a ruffled collar, not a bow."

"It's an Akita. And you'll be pleased to know you're saving a life." Trish brought her hand melodramatically to her heart. And accidentally let go of the leash. The dog scooted nervously within the group. Everyone took a nervous step back, except for Jason.

He squatted on his haunches. "Here, boy. Atta boy." He whistled softly. He held out his hand, palm side up.

The dog seemed to relax a little. He ventured a sniff.

"See, you can always tell a country boy." Vernon smiled, clearly glad to pass the buck where large animals were concerned. "Why don't you do that funny little snickering noise they always make in cowboy movies?"

"Vernon, he's a dog, not a palomino," Jason said. He tried coaxing the dog forward.

"Someone should grab his leash," Claire's mother announced, making no move to do it herself.

Classic, thought Claire. She bent to pick up the end of

the leash just when the Akita lurched to the right. She was too late. Jason's lightning quick reflexes weren't fast enough, either. He missed the dog, missed the leash, brushing Claire's hand instead. Claire felt the flash of heat. She rose instantly, not daring to look in his eyes. She looked around for the dog.

It had come to rest.

Relieving itself on Claire's mother's leg.

And Claire did what she always did.

She took the picture.

13

"CLAIRE, DID YOU SEE? He hardly noticed me?" Trish was sitting on the bed of her room, crying. Despite its waterproof claims, her mascara had run in blotches, giving her a certain plaguelike look.

"You're overreacting. David was delighted to see you." Claire sat next to her. She tried blotting the smudges with some tissues, but it only seemed to make matters worse. And now was definitely not the time to ask where Trish kept her eye makeup remover.

"Do you really think so?" Trish sniffed and hiccuped.

"I'm sure of it." Especially since you brought Jason, Claire thought, though she had the good sense not to mention that out loud.

"I think you're right." Trish breathed in deeply and closed her eyes. Then she opened them and slumped the way a thirteen-year-old girl does when she's embarrassed about developing breasts. "Oh, who am I kidding?" She threw the wad of wet tissues at the wastepaper basket by the side of the bed. It was wicker, trimmed in eyelet and gingham ribbon. "The only person he was interested in was Jason. Even Natalie didn't stand a chance. And I so wanted to make an impression."

"Trust me. You made an impression." It would have been hard not to make an impression—between the backless dress, sports superstar escort and a small bearlike dog who, after dousing her mother's leg, ran in clockwise circles around the open bar until he succumbed to Jason's charms and a piece of liverwurst. But then who wouldn't have succumbed? To Jason's charms, that is.

Ah, her hero. Everybody's hero. Right now he had agreed to have an after-dinner drink with David and a number of other male wedding guests at a bar in town. No doubt he was politely listening as they regaled him with their own tales of athletic derring-do. Then just as politely, he'd autograph cocktail napkins—his name conjoined with a dancing frog—now there was a collector's item. He'd agree to meet with their nephews, grandsons and pen pals from Peoria in the locker room. And how many free tickets would he consent to distribute?

No wonder Vernon wanted to monitor the situation. And this was just with the men. What happened with the women who wanted to know all about his love life? Or who wanted to be part of his love life? Was this what life was constantly like for Jason? Demands on his time? His attention? His wallet?

Didn't it all annoy him? Actually, when she thought about it, he seemed to enjoy it. Maybe it was a power thing—all that love and adoration. Maybe he just liked having beautiful blondes lying in wait, ready to pounce. Come to think of it, how many males would turn that down?

But was that the kind of life she was prepared for, especially when she would experience only the inconveniences and none of the adulation? She was in love, very much in love with Jason. She knew that now. And if it meant she had to share him with gazillions of strangers, she told herself she could do it, provided all that outpouring of attention didn't go to his head—and it hadn't seemed to—and that it didn't last forever. She wanted to be able to curl up in front of the fireplace at home on a

Sunday morning and not worry that someone would stick a camera lens through the window and take pictures of her in old flannel pajamas and dirty hair, with headlines blaring the next day, Jason Doyle Declares, "Help! I've Married An Alien."

And what does he want? she wondered.

"What does who want?" Trish asked.

Claire blinked. She must have voiced her question out loud. "The desk clerk," she said quickly. "What does he want you to do with the dog?" They could hear it scratching at the bathroom door, where he had been banished. It turned out that David was allergic to dog dander, and he would not be able to keep the Akita. "How was I to know?" Trish had wailed, marking the initial assault on her mascara.

"The clerk insists that the inn's policy is no animals. For the amount of money they're making off this wedding, you'd think they'd bend the rules a little."

"You'd think they'd be sympathetic, with a name like the Dancing Frog." Claire tried to lighten the situation.

Trish didn't seem to get the joke. "Mr. Bruckner volunteered to take it," she said.

"Mr. Bruckner is really sweet these days." Claire thought of the hug. Had her father ever hugged her that way?

"Yes, he is. But Mrs. Bruckner nixed the dog. She says their cat would go crazy. And since the cat's been around for fourteen years, it has priority. I'm not sure that's a valid argument, do you?"

Claire didn't want to go there. "Did you try calling your parents?"

"I've tried calling, but I can't seem to reach them." She smiled bravely. "What about your mother?"

"My mother? Are you crazy? After the way it lifted its

leg on my mother's Bally shoes. She paid full price for those, too."

Trish looked over. "That's right. Your mother buys retail, doesn't she?"

Claire nodded.

"Yes, I can see how that could be a problem." She dropped her head with a thunk to her chest. It looked like she might start to cry again.

Claire sidled closer on the bed. "Do you want me to stay with you tonight?" she asked, putting her arm around Trish's shoulder. "Vernon can bunk with Jason in my room."

Trish lifted her head. "Don't be silly." She slowly unfurled her body and improved her posture to a truly magnificent state. She looked like the Statue of Liberty and Gina Lollobrigida in her younger days—much younger days—all rolled into one. "A girl needs a little pick-me-up at times like this. And I know just the pick-me-up." And her smile wasn't one little bit sweet.

"Jason, this is a disaster." Claire corralled Jason on the veranda.

"If you can put your arms around me, it can't be that much of a disaster." He looked around to see if they were alone. Not spotting anyone, he maneuvered her to a dark corner of the porch and pulled her close.

The kiss was deep, unrushed. Her toes were so relaxed when they finished that Claire felt she had just discovered some reverse form of reflexology. She dropped her forehead to his chest, breathing in deeply, savoring his strength. She was comforted and aroused all at the same time, a seeming contradiction—kind of like eating a chocolate-fudge sundae and finding you'd lost weight after all.

He nuzzled her neck. "See? How bad can things be?"

She closed her eyes. "Things are bad?"

"I don't know for sure, but you seemed to mention something about a disaster. Maybe it has something to do with the frosty reception earlier? Siberia is a tropical resort by comparison."

"Yes, it was hardly a Norman Rockwell gathering."

"How's Natalie doing? I was a little worried when Dave suggested we go out. I had visions of coming back to find her submerged in the punch bowl."

"Right after you left, she grabbed a bottle of champagne and announced she was going to her room." Claire puzzled. "You don't think she was going to do something other than drink it, do you? Normally, I wouldn't have such thoughts, but after tonight, I don't know. Anything's possible."

"You're telling me. Until now, I never would have thought you could fit a dog and two bags behind the driver's seat of a Porsche." Jason kissed her softly on the top of her head. "Poor boy, where is the fellow now anyway?"

"He's holed up in Trish's bathroom surrounded by complimentary soaps, hair conditioner and shoe shine cloths."

"That alone is enough to scare any dog. When you think about it, you can hardly blame him for wetting the floor."

"It wasn't just the floor. It was my mother you're talking about."

"Ah, yes. Your mother," he said knowingly.

Claire wasn't sure what and how much she should say. "Listen, I'm sorry for you about my mother." Sheila had quizzed Jason about his relationship with Trish with the rabid intensity of a political correspondent for the *Wash-*

ington Post determined to uncover a big story, get a front-page banner headline, and win a Pulitzer, all before midnight. "She can be a little insistent. I didn't know she'd be here."

"Don't worry. I'm just sorry for you." He held her more tightly.

"Oh, it's okay. In some weird way, I think she was actually trying to be nice."

"Some really weird way." He emphasized "really." He shifted his hands to her waist, and leaned her back. "You know, I think the best way for us to get over the tension of the evening would be to get down and get dirty."

Claire smiled. "Are you suggesting mud wrestling?"

"Are you?"

"I'm not sure mud wrestling really goes with The Dancing Frog motif."

"Too bad." He looked genuinely disappointed. "In that case, we'll just have to kick Vernon out of your room—believe me, he'll understand, it's a guy thing—and take advantage of the king-size bed."

"Actually, it's two queens," Claire corrected.

"Not to worry. I'm flexible. You'd be surprised at just how flexible." He quickly raised and lowered his eyebrows.

"Somehow that doesn't surprise me at all." Claire was already envisioning a number of coupling positions to test the strength of the sheets' hospital corners. And it hit her. "But what about Trish? You're supposed to be here as her fiancé."

"Believe me, I can be discreet when it comes to entering and exiting hotel rooms."

Claire frowned. "Why do I not want to hear any specific details?"

"Jealous?" He kissed her on the tip of her nose.

She waved him away. "I'm not so much concerned about the other guests. It's Trish who worries me. She's so upset. She was talking about doing something desperate."

"Oh, yeah? How desperate?"

"Bluntly put, she's looking to drown her sorrows in a quick lay."

"Anyone in particular?"

Claire gave him the eye.

"Oh, yeah? Trish mentioned me?"

"Not in so many words, but the meaning was clear."

"Me, huh?" Jason nodded thoughtfully. "That dress she was wearing was something, wasn't it? I wonder how it comes off?"

Claire bopped him on the shoulder. "Trust me, you've seen one zipper, you've seen them all." She paused. "And she's not just after a one-night stand."

Jason cocked his head. "She wants a nooner, too?"

"More like morning, noon and night. Trish has decided that you have great possibilities for being Mr. Right."

"What about Dave? I thought she was still pining away?"

"I think she shifted focus from winning him back to making him sorry about what he let get away."

"Ah, revenge is a motive that a man can relate to."

"That being the case, I think you should go talk to her."

Jason smirked. "I like that idea. Especially considering that red dress. I'm not so sure about that zipper theory of yours."

"If I didn't know better, I'd worry that you weren't merely kidding. Wait a minute." She peered at him closely. "You are just going to talk, right? I mean, I know we haven't established what you'd call a real working relationship or anything." Her words became less assured. "But I kind of assumed—" Words failed her. "Oh, I can't talk about stuff like this on a porch of an inn, in plain view of Saabs with vanity plates."

Jason caressed her cheek. "Claire, honey, you've got to learn to relax, enjoy the moment. Don't overthink the situation. Trust me, it doesn't pay."

"Okay, I guess," she said. Only she wasn't okay. She wasn't confident enough in herself, in her feelings for Jason, and especially his feelings for her.

"Trust me." He rubbed her ear gently.

It felt so good. But was that a reason to trust him? Claire had no experience with getting close enough to anyone to develop a sense of trust.

He bent and kissed her lightly on the lips. "And now, my dear, I'm off to the rescue." He stepped back and saluted her. "Wish me luck. I'll be back as soon as possible to sweep you off your feet. And maybe do something else to your feet, as well." He sighed dramatically. "It's a cruel world, but a man's got to do what a man's got to do." He charged through the door and into the lobby.

CLAIRE WAITED in a rocking chair on the veranda.

She had no trouble spotting the windows for her room and Trish's. The light was on in hers. She could make out the blur of people moving.

Some minutes passed. She clutched her sides. The night air had grown chilly, and her black dress while supremely practical when it came to washing provided very little protection against the elements. She rocked more vigorously and stared at the window.

Now it looked as if there might be only one person moving around in her room. Had Jason left? The light was still on. Had Vernon understood the situation? Had he said, "Way to go, buddy. She's a great gal! I knew she was the one for you from the word go. Don't let her get away, whatever you do." Or words to that effect. After tonight's performance at the dinner, Claire had newly found respect for Vernon's people skills. Or maybe he just had plenty of experience dealing with dysfunctional types.

Claire was getting seriously chilled. And no amount of rocking could hold it off any longer. She hurried into the front parlor—filled with overstuffed chintz-covered love seats, a rolltop desk with fountain pen set and, of course, Dancing Frog stationery, bookshelves lined with a complete selection of the works of Jane Austen, and a wooden newspaper stand containing *Town & Country*. The crackling fire was tempting, but the rendezvous point was outside, and she didn't want to risk missing Jason.

She grabbed a mohair throw—green, what else?—and hoped it wouldn't admit some loud beep when she took it through the front door. It didn't.

Claire cuddled up in the chair again, tucking her feet underneath. She wrapped the throw closely around her shoulders and looked up. The light in her room was off. She looked down three windows to Trish's room. She could tell the light was on, but the heavy curtains were drawn, so she couldn't make out what was going on. Not to worry. Claire snuck her hand from under the throw and looked at her watch. He'd be down pretty soon, she told herself. She rocked.

And she rocked. Twenty minutes later, she was still rocking. Lights went on in more rooms. Some went off. Hers came on. Went off again.

She rocked. Thirty-four minutes later she was still

rocking. More lights went off. One that hadn't been on before, came on suddenly. The inn of the Dancing Frog was hopping, literally. Claire turned her head and listened. Yes, she heard croaking.

She checked her watch again. Forty-seven minutes and counting. By now her already cold-prone fingers were numb. No amount of rubbing seemed to restore circulation. Her right foot had fallen asleep, and she was getting a crick in her neck from craning to peer into the windows.

She rocked. And then she stopped rocking. She unfolded her legs and planted them on the wooden floor. She looked at her watch. Again. Fifty-four minutes. She frowned. Something must be wrong.

Maybe Trish had become hysterical? Had been inconsolable? Decided after all that she wanted David and had thrown herself on him, only to have Natalie draw a gun. Jason, who must have run into the fray, got in the line of fire and had been shot. Right now, he could be lying there, trying to speak her name with his last breath.

No, don't be ridiculous, she told herself. She would have heard a gunshot. Or would she? The croaking was pretty loud. It could muffle the sound, especially if the gun had a silencer. Or maybe it wasn't a gun. Maybe Natalie had pulled out some lethal orthodontic tool and stabbed Jason accidentally in the heart. Vernon would be holding his bleeding body, a cell phone tucked under his chin as he called 911, and Natalie would be clutching the murder weapon, weeping, "I'm so sorry. And he had such perfect teeth."

Claire shook her head. The cold was clearly affecting her brain. There had to be a much simpler explanation for the delay. She looked to Trish's room again. It looked as though a light was still on, but maybe not as bright.

Had the overhead fixture been turned off, leaving only the bedside light on?

And that's when Claire really started to worry. Maybe Jason was doing what a man usually did?

WHEN SHE REACHED the top step of the stairway, Claire heard a door slam. She stopped. Listened. But didn't hear anything else. She let go of the polished banister and stepped onto the carpet runner in the hallway. A lithograph of some barnyard theme greeted her. A cow was looking over its shoulder, ostensibly at a fly biting its haunch, but Claire could tell the bovine was really watching the late-night comings and goings. On the table under the picture was a crocheted thingamabob on top of which sat a brass bowl with dried hydrangeas. Someone had tipped an empty champagne bottle into the flower arrangement. No wonder the cow was skeptical.

Claire looked to her left, down the hallway. She saw David quickly rush up a side stairway. He was carrying towels and extra bedding. He opened a door and closed it behind him. Did he need to stanch the blood? No, it was far more likely that Natalie had kicked him out of her room and he was camping out elsewhere.

She slowly walked down the hall. Her room was on the right, three doors down. She put the heavy key in the door and slowly turned the handle. She opened the door and walked in. It was dark, except for the hallway light spilling in on the needlework rug. She hesitated. She flipped the light switch on the wall and shut the door behind her. She looked around. The beds were turned down. A complimentary chocolate lay on her pillow. Her bag was open on the luggage rack at the foot of her bed. She looked in the armoire. Her clothes still hung there. Her camera bag still lay propped against the desk chair.

She turned to look at the other bed more closely. No chocolate. But Vernon's garment bag rested unopened at the end. He had been here. But he wasn't here now. Was he coming back? Claire circled around the room, looking for more clues.

She heard a door open down the hallway. She tiptoed to the door and opened it a crack. She couldn't see a thing. She pulled the door open a little wider and peeked around the edge.

She saw her mother. She was leaving a room—Mr. Bruckner's room. Mr. Bruckner's room! Claire covered her mouth and looked again. Yes, it definitely was her mother, and she'd discarded the short jacket that went with her cocktail dress. Her dress was sleeveless. Her mother never exposed her upper arms in public—she was very conscious of incipient underarm flab.

Sheila carried a bottle of champagne. And she was giggling. And she buzzed Mr. Bruckner on the lips. Her mother?

She was padding this way so Claire closed her door, stopping before it clicked shut. She listened to the sound of footsteps. Claire dared to open her door again and saw her mother knock on another door. And, my God, she wasn't wearing shoes. Claire had never seen her mother not wearing shoes. She sometimes wondered if her mother showered in shoes.

The door opened in front of her mother. A woman's arm jutted out. It was bare. And it definitely waddled in the underarm area. Claire gulped. No! Yes! It was Mrs. Bruckner, and she was pulling her mother into her room. It was unbelievable to think of her mother with Mr. Bruckner. But what was she doing with Mrs. Bruckner now? Her mother couldn't possibly be involved in a ménage à trois, could she? She had to find Jason. Tell him what she saw.

She opened the door wider to step out into the hall when another door opened farther down the hallway. Trish's door. Claire quickly stepped back into her room and closed the door far enough that she could still see but no one would know her door was ajar.

It was Jason. Thank goodness. He wasn't dead. He looked very much in one piece.

And there was a lot of that piece showing.

Claire was wide-eyed. He didn't have on a jacket. Or a shirt for that matter. The mellow hall light glinted off his dark hair, illuminating the curls on his chest, and accentuating the muscles of his arms. He was looking up and down the hall.

And then she heard a voice. Trish's voice. "Is anyone out there?"

He looked up and down again.

"I was sure I heard a door open and shut," Trish whispered from inside the room.

Jason shook his head. "Well, there may have been someone out here, but the coast is clear now." He looked back into her room.

"Then quick, hurry back in. We've got just enough time before somebody finds out. And you know who I mean." Trish's voice was more insistent. Louder. She must have moved closer to Jason.

Claire saw a naked arm reach out for Jason's shoulder. No, it wasn't completely naked. A skinny little black negligee strap fell insouciantly over her upper arm. And believe me, there wasn't a waddle in sight.

Claire didn't wait to see any more. She pulled back and silently shut her door. She rested her forehead against the heavy wood. How long she stood like that she couldn't say for sure. Long enough that her calves started to hurt from not moving.

She turned around, and leaning against the door, stared sightlessly around the room. She slid slowly to the floor and let her arms rest on her knees.

She stayed that way until just before daybreak, when she pulled herself together. She showered and dressed, and clutching her camera close, stole outside.

Jason never returned.

14

CLAIRE WASN'T SURE HOW she did it. It was truly amazing.

More amazing was that there was a wedding at all.

Even more amazing was that everybody looked happy. Sublimely happy.

True, Natalie did look a little green around the gills when she and the groom exchanged vows. But when they had turned to face each other as the minister announced, "You may kiss the bride," the smooch that ensued definitely involved a sharing of bodily fluids.

Natalie could have removed a few fillings. And David. Never had Claire seen so much passion displayed by a district attorney, let alone a boy from Leeds Springs. Residents of that tiny hamlet tended to shake hands, nod briskly, and at most, kiss one cheek—never two, too European.

Claire was amazed at the passionate embrace. But she took the picture.

And when she turned to face the guests, sitting in little white chairs lined up neatly on the parquet wood floor of the Bruckners's grand dining room—the mammoth Spanish Baroque dining room table and chairs had been disassembled and moved to the bedrooms upstairs and the mansion-size Shiraz carpet rolled up and carted to the library—she saw an enormous and totally uncharacteristic public display of affection. Hanky-panky seemed to have a way of bringing people out of their customarily restrictive shells.

Mr. Bruckner was kissing Mrs. Bruckner, who was crying at the same time. Her mother held hands with her stepfather and rested her head on his shoulder. It wasn't exactly passionate, but given the range of emotions that her mother usually operated in, it verged on flamenco-like fire. Maybe this is what exercising your options both ways could stir up?

Claire was stunned. But needless to say, she kept taking pictures.

Trish and Jason sat next to each other a few rows back, with Vernon on Trish's other side. Jason slipped his hand into Trish's. It rested on her lap. She turned and winked. He turned. And kissed her cheek. He murmured something close up. She smiled. Knowingly. The corner of his mouth turned up. She smiled more. Arched her eyebrows, then leaned over to say something to Vernon. Her breasts pushed against the purple-brown slip dress that was provocatively visible under a loose, gauzy, smock-like overtop.

Claire watched as Trish turned back to Jason and tendered him a light kiss on the cheek. She felt her stomach turn.

For once, she didn't take the picture.

After the ceremony was completed, Claire was busy taking the family portraits. The rest of the guests meandered out to the tent, which was set up off the bluestone patio and accessed from the dining room by the wall of French doors. The sounds of Cole Porter mingled with the clinking of glasses and the voices of two hundred and fifty or so of only the closest family and friends.

Claire chatted reassuringly with David and Natalie and the family members from both sides. "I only take pictures that make the women look thin and the men look handsome," she told them with a straight face.

First, she posed Natalie and David. No need to ask them to cuddle closer. They instantly grabbed each other's hands and gazed into each other's eyes. They had the look. Claire saw it. They really were in love, despite everything. Maybe there was hope for eternal happiness after all. She doubted it, but then, what did she know? She was just the photographer, as she always liked to say. And given her recent experiences, maybe that was the safest position to be in.

She changed film rolls and orchestrated the various arrangements of the wedding party, including the best man—a colleague of David's from Chicago who had an inability to look straight into the camera—and the matron of honor—Natalie's older sister from Bethesda, seven months pregnant. Claire told them how great they all looked. A lie—Natalie's dress was a little too much *Gone With the Wind* for her taste, and the bridesmaids would have a tough time recycling their dresses—how many places can you wear candy-cane pink satin gowns?—but they all truly looked happy. The fashion police would have to wait outside. Then came the in-laws, alone and with the newlyweds. It was a symphony of hair spray and support-top panty hose.

Thirty minutes later, the major players drifted into the tent. The waiters moved briskly. The orchestra took a break from "Night and Day" and "I Get a Kick Out of You." The salad of arugula with walnuts, poached pears and crumbled Stilton gave way to salmon in a sour cream-dill sauce. Somewhere between the first and second course, the best man rose and toasted the groom.

Claire crisscrossed the floor, working the tables to get informal photos. Professional that she was, she approached the table where her mother, stepfather and another woman were sitting.

"Hello, Mother." She leaned over and kissed her mother's powdered cheek. "William." She nodded to her stepfather. He saluted with a tumbler generously filled with amber-colored liquid.

"That's my daughter," she heard her mother say. "You remember Mrs. Hornung, don't you, Claire?" Great. Her mother and her old history teacher. She would need several cloves of garlic and a large wooden stake to fend off the pair of them.

Instead she smiled sweetly, reverting to being seventeen years old. "Hello, Mrs. Hornung. Could I get a picture of you lovely ladies reminiscing about old times?"

"Not that old," her mother said archly.

"Just pleasantly aged." Her stepfather smiled.

"No drinks in the picture, dear," her mother replied tartly.

"Smiles, now. Nothing but good memories." Claire focused the camera.

"I'm not sure I have any good memories," Mrs. Hornung said through a tense smile.

"That's great." Claire took the picture and stepped back. "Thank you so much. David and Natalie said they wanted a picture of you especially." She had been saying the same thing to every table she visited.

"I bet she says that to all the tables," Mrs. Hornung said.

"Claire, wait a minute, dear." Her mother gave a royal wave.

Claire abased herself at her feet. "Yes?"

"That outfit is very nice." Claire wore the same black dress as last night, but she'd paired it with a matching three-quarter-length vest in gray with a thin black stripe at the bottom. "Isn't it clever the way you can recycle the same dress two days in a row," her mother said.

Ouch. "Did you see I wore your lipstick?" Claire replied, trying to be the good daughter, a losing cause, but a cause nonetheless.

Her mother patted her hand. "I did. And it makes a big difference."

A losing cause for sure.

By the cutting of the cake, Claire had taken all the required "event" shots except for the first dance. She had seriously worked all the tables. But one. She'd get to it. She really would.

But as the orchestra tuned up and started to play "Cherish"—"Cherish"? Whose idea had that been?—she quickly circled the temporary dance floor to get the bride and groom doing a halting fox trot.

She focused. And took the picture.

The couple's sweet ineptness proved contagious. The large quantities of good champagne consumed probably helped, too. Not to mention the room-swapping antics of the bridal party last night at the inn—talk about coupling. All that must have loosened inhibitions. Beyond that, Claire didn't want to think about what exactly was loosened.

In any case, with all this uncharacteristic display of enthusiasm, the orchestra, used to having only a token flower girl on Ritalin and a sloshed maternal uncle dancing to their melodies—"Isn't that cute," everyone would say to the person sitting next to them—got into the swing of things. Here in the middle of discreet WASPdom, the guests were positively getting down, swaying to the de-lightful, de-licious dance music.

Stranger things had happened, Claire thought. In any

case, it made for good photos. Especially of you-know-who.

Jason was working overtime. He squired Trish for the requisite number of dances, then moved on to Natalie and Mrs. Bruckner. Next, he gave her mother a twirl—brave man—or fool, depending on your frame of reference. Despite his size, he moved with an easy grace. Why wasn't Claire surprised? He did everything physical with an almost sublime ease. Everything. She shivered, remembering just how sublime.

The band struck up "I've Got My Love to Keep Me Warm." And that's when it was as if Moses had parted the waters.

A male voice greeted her from behind. "You've got to get a shot of that." It was David talking to her.

Claire was too busy picking her jaw up off the floor to answer. If taking pictures were not as automatic as breathing, she never would have been able to raise her camera and shoot.

Jason was dancing with Mrs. Hornung. She was pulling him closer and leading as only a high school American history teacher can.

David whistled. "I knew he was no ordinary man. But now I know he is immortal."

Stunned, Claire kept taking pictures.

"I'm sure this must qualify for Ripley's Believe It or Not! I just can't figure out how," David continued to marvel.

She finished the roll and reached into the pocket of the vest for another. She looked down to reload.

"And now the gods have decided to shine down upon us," David said.

Claire looked up. But she didn't have to.

She already knew who was coming their way.

Jason approached. The look in his eye was unmistakable. He might ostensibly be asking her to dance, but it was sex that he was after.

Claire felt the same reaction she'd felt that first day outside Madison Square Garden. He was to die for. With his tuxedo jacket open and his bow tie loosened, Jason was a picture of sophistication ready to be sullied and sully in kind. The ebony studs on his dress shirt gleamed. The dimple creased his cheek. His eyes narrowed. The scar winked.

Here was the perfect man—but not for her, damn it.

He strode toward her more purposely, shaking off a waiter carrying a tray of champagne glasses.

David looked from Jason to Claire. "Why do I get the feeling he hasn't come to talk about this year's crop of rookies?"

Claire didn't reply. Neither did Jason.

About three feet away he stopped, put his hands into the side pockets of his trousers, and rocked back on his heels. And let the corner of his mouth barely rise.

If it were a cartoon, a Danger sign would start to flash.

Only Jason wasn't some cartoon action hero.

He was flesh and blood, with an emphasis on hard flesh and hot blood.

And Claire did what she always did.

She took the picture.

David cleared his throat. "Can I get anyone anything?" he asked, his voice a little squeaky.

"I think we're just fine," Jason drawled, something Claire never would have thought possible for someone born and bred in the Granite State.

David looked back and forth between the two of them. "Well, I think I may need something. If you'll excuse me." He hadn't gotten to be a Chicago D.A. on looks alone.

Jason waited for David to leave. "Care to join me in a dance?" He held out his hand.

Claire pointed to her camera. "Working girl here."

"You know what they say, all work and no play makes—"

"A girl healthy, wealthy and wise?" Claire finished his sentence.

"That wasn't my first choice, but I can fully appreciate strong, accomplished women. Still, you wanna dance?" He cocked his head to the activity behind him. The orchestra was belting out a spirited rendition of "Is That All There Is."

Claire held up her hand. "I have a confession to make. I don't really like to dance."

"You're kidding me?"

She shook her head.

Jason smiled broadly. "You realize you've just fulfilled yet another requirement for a future perfect wife. You must be the only woman in the world who doesn't like to dance. A great weight has been lifted from my shoulders. I no longer feel the need to impress you with my abilities to waltz without bumping into people or furniture."

Claire grunted.

"That was supposed to be a joke."

"That was supposed to be a laugh."

Jason took his hands out of his pockets and came closer. "Is this about last night?" he asked softly. "I'm sorry we couldn't get together. Things got a little crazy."

"That's one way to describe the situation." Her voice was sarcastic and ugly. She didn't like the sound of it, but she was too hurt to cover it up.

"Wait a minute, don't prejudge me. I've been wanting

to talk to you, but frankly, I haven't had a free moment up until now."

"It must be tough having to be at the beck and call of a beautiful woman."

"I'm going to ignore that comment because I know you don't mean it." He reached out to stroke her arm.

She pulled back. "You know, do you?"

The laughter was completely gone from his voice. "If it makes you feel any better, I'd be happy to give you the gruesome details on last night—"

Claire held up her hand. "Please, spare me. Besides, last night is history."

"One some of us would prefer to forget, believe me," Jason said quickly.

So it hadn't been bliss between the sheets. Claire felt somewhat vindicated. Only somewhat. "What I prefer to talk about is today, the here and now," she said, moving on to the topic that she really wanted to address.

Jason seemed relieved. "Thank goodness. Now you've come around to my way of thinking. Can we just enjoy the moment?"

Claire pursed her lips. "I'm not sure enjoyment is at the top of my list at this moment." She fingered her camera nervously. It was time to fess up to her feelings and to probe him about his, no matter how painful.

Jason reached for her camera.

She held on to the strap.

"C'mon. Fork it over." He motioned with his fingers. "We need to talk, and I'm not going to let you hide behind that thing any longer. You know, sometimes I hate that camera." He reached out for the strap again.

She thought a moment. She didn't want to create a scene, so she let him ease it off her shoulder.

He slung it over his without even thinking. "Okay,

clearly you've got something on your mind. So out with it."

Claire stared at him. It was incredibly irritating to see her camera, her dad's camera, hanging from Jason's shoulder. He looked so comfortable with the weight, and it looked so right there. It made her all the more furious.

"Jason, do you ever think about more than today?" she asked, hands on hips.

"Well, at the moment, I'm trying hard to ignore the bad feelings of the moment and concentrate on the great feelings I'm sure we'll manage to make together tonight."

Claire stared at the tent ceiling. Garlands of white, pink and magenta hibiscus brought a bit of the West Indies to Westchester. She looked down. "Jason, I love you." There she said it.

She was greeted by silence.

"Any reaction to the news?" she prompted him.

"Wow." He rubbed the side of his head. "I mean it. Wow."

"Is that a 'wow' good or a 'wow' bad?"

"It's a wow. What kind I really can't say. In fact, I don't know what to say in general." He groped for words. "I'm flattered. You're a fantastic woman. You're talented, beautiful, unique."

She pursed her lips. "Why do I get the feeling that there's a 'but' coming?"

"I'm sorry. I just haven't been thinking along those lines. I'm one of those people who lives for the moment. I don't tend to analyze my feelings. I just go with what feels right."

"Feels right?" She was indignant. "Feels right?" She wasn't asking him whether he wanted his back scratched.

Jason nodded. "That's right. What feels right," he said firmly.

Claire held up her hands and thought a minute before speaking. "I'm sorry. You just can't go through life strictly doing what feels right. You need to think about the consequences or the deeper motives behind your actions."

"What are you getting at?"

"Take the whole need-for-speed hang-up you've got."

"All guys like fast cars. What's wrong with that?"

"What's wrong with that? A hockey team has just laid out millions of dollars to help boost its ticket sales and chances for a play-off berth, and you don't find it selfish that you put yourself at risk by zooming around Manhattan and greater New Jersey?"

Jason held up his hands. "I think something else is going on here besides the fact that I happen to like fast cars and bikes. I think the real issue is that you equate my lifestyle with selfishness. No, you think it's more than selfish. You think it's dangerous."

"I don't know what you're talking about?" Of course she did.

"Of course you do. You see danger and you immediately think death."

Claire opened her mouth to speak.

"No, don't interrupt," Jason warned her. "It's my turn now. Let's take the example of your father, the great Jim Marsden, your idol. He loved living on the edge, taking risks. Where did that leave you at a young age? Fatherless."

Claire didn't deny it. She couldn't.

"Now, do I need to analyze your decision to give up news photography?" Jason continued. "Might it have something to do with fear? Fear of people—including yourself—constantly being at risk? Constantly facing the very real possibility of danger? Claire, I don't live in some war-torn part of the world. I am merely enjoying life. I don't intend to curtail my lifestyle just to assuage your fear of death. It doesn't make any sense."

Claire inhaled deeply. "Okay, maybe you're right. Maybe I do have a hang-up. But I'm not the only one with a problem." They had gotten to a point where she wasn't about to hold anything back. "You tout this live-for-the-day mentality. Well, I think you do because you're scared, just as scared as I am." She poked him in the chest. "I think you're scared that you're not immortal. That if you stop to think about the future, you'll see that your life as a sports star is limited. That the cheering is going to end."

"Are you finished?" Jason said very softly.

"Not quite. Before you jump on me, just remember that your friends are telling you the same thing," she said.

"I don't know what you mean."

"Don't play dumb with me, Jason Doyle. That's one of your favorite games, isn't it—playing the dumb jock? It allows you to avoid thinking about the future. Tell me, what is Simone always on about? What does she want you to finish?"

"Medical school," he grumbled.

"Medical school?" She was incredulous. No, she wasn't. He had gone to a top-rate university and majored in biology. She nodded in sudden understanding. "Now I get it. The physiology book or whatever it was. Larry. That day at the hospital—he wasn't talking about the foundation, he was talking about medical school." She snapped her fingers. "And that time at the university gym. I bet you know about it because you're taking courses or are going to take courses there. Am I right?"

"That's enough," Jason warned.

"Oh, sorry, mustn't let out the secret that Jason Doyle goes to medical school. Might ruin his image as a fun-loving jock."

"I've just taken a few courses here and there. I'm hardly a full-time student."

"And why is that?"

"Maybe it has something to do with the fact that I am a full-time professional hockey player." Now his voice was harsh.

"You have an off season, don't you? Other players have finished degrees when they're not playing." Claire folded her arms across her chest and eyed him critically. "No, I think that's an excuse. An excuse to keep you from planning for the future, making a commitment, any kind of commitment."

She unfolded her arms and stepped forward. She yanked her camera off his shoulder, not caring that it swung and clipped her in the side. "Give me back my camera. I think I prefer being behind it, especially where you're concerned."

15

TWO WEEKS LATER Claire slouched in a chair in Trish's office and toyed with the shoelace of her hiking boot.

Trish was smartly attired in a vintage red, bias-cut sheath—very Edith Head. She even had a matching turban with a gi-normous brooch. Claire sure hoped the plum-size stone in the middle was fake. Otherwise some poor piece of rock had died for an ignoble cause.

Trish's carefully lacquered fingernails tapped on the most recent issue of *Focus*. Their vermilion color matched the color of her lips.

"My mother would approve of your lipstick," Claire said.

"You don't know how happy that makes me feel. But enough chitchat. Have you seen the figures?" She was referring to the latest issue of the magazine.

Claire uncrossed her legs and recrossed them the other way around. "No, I just got in from L.A., shooting the Malibu piece you assigned me, remember?"

"We set a new newsstand sales record."

"I'm delighted." Claire picked at the hem of her jeans.

Trish tapped the magazine again. "Frankly, with this cover, we could have run the Hastings-on-Hudson Yellow Pages and broken the record for most copies sold."

Claire inclined her chin and acknowledged the cover. It was a shot of Jason. Not just any shot. It was from the wedding. When he'd approached her to dance.

Any woman who saw the cover wasn't thinking soft-shoe.

Any man who picked up a copy wasn't contemplating slap shots.

They were thinking sex, sex, sex.

And as the sales figures proved—sex sells.

When Claire looked at the cover she could only think of one thing—sorrow, sorrow, sorrow.

Actually, for all she knew, *Focus* had published the Yellow Pages. She and Trish had spoken about the article in general terms and they had agreed on the choice of photos, but she hadn't had the heart to read the piece over once the issue had come out.

"Your cover art definitely made people pick up the issue, but Jason's story really sold it."

"You're a good writer," Claire said. It was true.

"No, for once I'm not talking about my skill," Trish said. "Jason's story was simply dynamite."

Claire offered a stiff smile. "I'm sure he's a regular Boy Scout."

Trish flipped to the appropriate pages. "Actually, he was an Eagle Scout. But I suppose you know all about his growing up?" She raised an eyebrow-penciled brow.

Claire shrugged. "I know he comes from some little town in Vermont and his mother ran a lumberyard, but that's about it."

"She just didn't run it. She owned it after Jason's father died of stomach cancer when Jason was nine." Trish looked at the story again. "No, ten, leaving him, his mother and three younger siblings. Jason shouldered most of the household duties so his mother could take over his father's business."

"He told you all of this?"

"No, of course not. Does that sound like something Jason would say?"

Claire shook her head. Jason had his faults, but you could never accuse him of going on about himself.

"I found out the details when I called up his younger sister Ginny. She went on and on about Big Brother. Even told me that he made a mean meatloaf. She explained how he helped them get to school, helped them with their homework, and worked in the lumberyard on weekends. Apparently, he earned a full scholarship to Grantham. But on school breaks, he still came home to help out. Even now, when he visits home, he works at the yard. His mother won't take a dime, but Ginny tells me how Jason has paid for one of her kids to be educated at private school. Seems he has severe dyslexia."

Claire slumped down in the armchair. "The guy sounds like a saint." And he was all Trish's.

"Absolutely perfect." Trish sighed. "Too bad." Though she didn't seem particularly heartbroken.

"Too bad?" Claire put both feet on the ground. "There's a problem?"

"The problem is, he's not the perfect guy for me. Though I'm sure he'd be perfect for someone else." Trish winked.

Trish winking? Or was it her mascara sticking? Claire was confused. Nothing seemed obvious to her. "And you found this out before or after you two hit the sack?" Was it fair that Claire had sacrificed Jason because of her friendship for Trish—okay, that wasn't entirely true—and now Trish decided he wasn't the one?

"What are you talking about?" Trish asked.

"I saw Jason go into your room. Without a shirt. The night before the wedding. And you had on some slinky nightgown or something."

Trish put her elbows on the edge of the desk and cupped her chin in her hands. "The reason Jason was without his shirt was because he had just come from helping David carry Natalie back to her room. She had drunk too much champagne and stupidly climbed out onto the window ledge running along the back of the inn. She wouldn't come in for David. She kept saying that he didn't love her anymore, had never loved her. So David came to my room looking for Jason. Anyway, to make a long story short, Jason went and managed to coax her in. Natalie rewarded Jason's gesture by throwing up all over him."

"Yuck." Still, she had seen him going into Trish's room. She'd listened, and the door had never reopened. "So he was a regular hero with Natalie. It still doesn't explain what he was doing in your room."

"He was helping Mr. Bruckner get the Akita out."

"What are you talking about? The Akita? I never heard him come out of your room again."

"Doing a little spying, were you?"

Claire waved her off. "So what if I was. You still haven't answered the question."

"Well, Nancy Drew, for your information, the bathroom to my room was connected to the Bruckners's room. They had booked into the hotel because the bedrooms at their house were already overflowing with furniture that they had moved to make room for the wedding."

"But I saw my mother going into Mr. Bruckner's room. And then into another room with Mrs. Bruckner." Claire still cringed at the thought.

Trish rolled her eyes. "She was helping out."

"My mother?" Claire squawked.

"Yes, she decided she liked the Akita and took pity on

it. The only problem was, she couldn't take it home because your stepfather is afraid of dogs." It was true. Claire knew that. "And seeing as he was stuck in Manhattan anyway, she agreed to stay and help distract Mrs. Bruckner so that Mr. Bruckner could sneak out with Jason and take the dog to their house."

"Dare I ask how my mother distracted Mrs. Bruckner?"

"She insisted that they needed to take over David's room, so that he would be forced to stay with Natalie all night and kiss and make up. I think those were your mother's exact words."

"And what did my mother and Mrs. Bruckner do all night?" Claire eyed her suspiciously.

"Apparently, they sat up drinking and playing strip poker. Since they both wear a full array of undergarments, I think only a minimum of flesh was ever exposed. I gather you can also count pieces of jewelry as separate items."

"They could have been there a week before taking off a stitch of clothing," Claire conceded. She paused. Then looked at Trish again. "So, you're telling me you didn't spend the night with some man?"

Trish grinned that stupid smile that was the true hallmark of a woman in love. "I didn't say that. I did. With Mr. Right."

Claire was totally confused. "If you're not talking about Jason, who are you talking about? Who was it you were with that night?"

Trish stretched her neck up regally. "Why, Vernon, of course."

Claire practically jumped out of the chair. "Vernon?" She thought a moment. "He did come through in the clutch that weekend, I'll give you that."

"Oh, he more than came through in the clutch. Trust me." Trish blushed, coordinating fully with her outfit. "He's so sweet, so understanding." Trish grinned that stupid grin that Claire was starting to recognize so well. "And so oral," she added.

Claire waved her hands in front of herself. "Why don't you save that for another time. I still want to know about David."

"What about him?"

"I thought you thought you were still in love with him, that you were upset that he didn't seem to care anymore?"

"Claire, Patti was in love with David. I'm not Patti."

"Yes, you are. You just go by a different name."

"No, trust me, I'm not the girl that Patti was. I'm a thirty-year-old woman with a responsible job, a healthy income, and my own apartment."

Claire could identify with the first two. And she really needed to do something about the third.

"And believe me." Trish leaned forward. "Unlike some people, I know what to do when I meet Mr. Right." She looked at Claire pointedly, and it wasn't to let her know her cuff was frayed.

CLAIRE WAS SITTING at a computer screen in the art department at *Focus*. She was working, cropping and finishing off photos. She had used one of the new digital cameras for the California story.

Two days ago she had listened to Trish lecture her. Well, she wasn't stupid—a little slow, but not stupid. It took her a day, but she had finally gotten the picture. She was a photographer, after all.

Not that it had done her any good so far.

Trish and Vernon had invited her to Sunday brunch at

some chic new watering hole. But rather than drown her sorrows in mimosas—and listen to them discuss the merits of lemongrass—Claire had decided to do some work. She had the place to herself. She slipped a CD into the boom box, and with earphones on, listened to Ella Fitzgerald and Louis Armstrong let loose with "Stompin' at the Savoy."

She was shaking and bobbing to the music, touching up a photo of a sixties TV star who had once been known for a limited emotional repertoire but remarkable set of pectorals. His action-adventure series had taken place in Hawaii, so the combination was perfect.

If only his pectorals had withstood the test of time. She worked the computer mouse carefully, concentrating on helping his body defy the forces of age and gravity. She squinted into the screen and tapped away as the music built to a crescendo.

Clunk.

Claire looked up, startled. Then she looked at the counter next to her. And nearly jumped out of her chair.

No, she did jump out of her chair. And found herself standing, with the cord of her earphones dangling free.

She blinked. Jason stood next to her. She pulled off the earphones and slid back into the chair. She didn't trust her legs.

"Apparently, this was delivered to me yesterday at the hotel. I was in Grantham and didn't get it until today. I think it might be yours." He pushed the box on the counter closer to her.

"No, I sent it to you. I don't need it anymore." She waved to the computer screen. "As you can see, I've gone digital, and I thought that since you're a new homeowner you might need a camera to take before-and-after pictures. Everybody says that they want to do that kind of thing, and then when the time comes, they don't have a camera and forget." She was rambling.

"You're rambling."

Claire rubbed her forehead. "I know." She smiled weakly.

Jason pulled out a chair from the terminal next to her and sat. He put an elbow on the desk and swiveled to face her. "Claire, why did you send me the camera?"

"I told you." She ran her fingertips nervously over the keyboard.

"Claire, why did you send me this camera?" he repeated in a quiet voice. He placed his hands on hers to stop the movement.

She didn't want to feel the warmth. Didn't want to feel the aching desire. She closed her eyes. And spoke the truth. "I sent you the camera, that particular camera, because I wanted to give it to you." She paused. This was harder than she had imagined. And she had imagined the worst.

"I sent it to you—" She gulped. "I sent it to you because I wanted you to see that I could come out from behind my camera, that camera. And I wanted to say that I'm sorry. Given the time we spent together, what we shared, I had assumed that you were thinking in the long term. Even the short term. But clearly I read the situation wrong." She took another deep breath. "Anyhow, I wish you lots of luck, now and in the future. Not that I'm saying you have to look into the future. It's your decision if you choose to look strictly in the present. I realize I am in no position to judge, especially after all the things you've been through in your life."

She opened her eyes and slowly turned her head to look at him. She hadn't become suddenly brave. She was still a coward. But she knew that it was time to face the truth.

He still didn't say anything. In fact, he looked puzzled.

"Am I making any sense here—about the significance of the camera, that is?" she asked.

Jason wrinkled his brow. "All that from one camera?"

"Well, you know what they say. One picture is worth a thousand words."

"That was more like a couple hundred."

Claire rolled her eyes. "A thousand, a hundred. Let's not get hung up on the details."

Jason reached over and rubbed his index finger across the back of her hand. She inhaled deeply.

"I find that paying attention to the details is extremely important for many things. For giving instructions to contractors."

"I can understand that." Her skin was acutely aware of the pressure he was applying.

"It's also crucial for arranging medical school courses around an already tight schedule, especially when you're trying to set some kind of timetable for completing a degree."

"I can understand that." The warmth in her hand had traveled up her arm and embraced her chest.

"It's also very important when you want to propose marriage in just the right way to the most incredible woman in the world."

Claire stopped breathing.

"You're not breathing."

She put her hand to her chest. He was right.

"Do you need mouth-to-mouth?" he asked.

She gulped. And nodded quickly.

Jason's version of a lifesaving maneuver might not correspond to proper Red Cross procedure, but it sure cured Claire's problems.

When they finished, he pulled back, but still held her in his arms. "You were right, Claire. I didn't want to think about the future because I didn't want to think about life out of the limelight. I'd had enough responsibilities growing up that I thought it was time I got to enjoy myself, let loose, not worry about what was to come. But I've come to realize that even a superjock has to think about the future, think about committing to something, someone for the future. And do you know how I know?"

There were tears in her eyes. "Because some photographer with this strange gray hair told you?"

Jason smiled. "That made a big difference, that's for sure. But the real clincher was Simone."

"Simone?" Claire smiled along with him. She could see where this was going.

"I can't let you get away. Simone's been bugging me so much—far worse than anything she says about medical school—that I can't take it anymore. Will you marry me?"

"You're proposing so you can get Simone to stop nagging you?"

"Hell, yes. It's my most important requirement for a perfect wife—someone who can get Simone off my back. You don't think that's a good qualification?"

Claire frowned in thought. "I must say, for once I can understand your priorities."

Jason rose and swept her up into his arms. "Ah, Claire, you're the greatest." He swung her around. Her feet fanned out. The pages of a large hanging calendar with inked-in photography assignments rippled with the movement of air. Her heels clipped the back of her chair and sent it rolling on its castors.

He brought her face to his and kissed her silly. They broke apart laughing.

"Just one thing." Claire was almost breathless.

"Anything."

"Could you say the magic words?"

"I'm sorry. Us dumb jocks have problems with open-ended questions."

Claire moaned.

Jason let her slide to the floor, the length of his body rubbing suggestively against hers. And believe me, no suggestions were needed. "Okay, here goes. Claire, even in my more extreme states of denial, I recognized your beauty, your intelligence, your talent, your wit. You are everything I could possibly want or ever need in a woman. You're challenging. Fun. Sexy as all get-out. And you're clearly the most tolerant. Only you could have forgiven me my denseness when it came to grasping my true feelings." He shook his head. "No, tolerance isn't the right word."

"It's not? I kind of like tolerance." Claire smiled.

"Tolerance is good, but it's not enough. It's courage. Your courage to admit your feelings, thereby making me realize mine. I love you, Claire. And if you don't know that by now, you're not the person I think you are."

"Why, I'm just the photographer."

He bent to kiss her again. "And that's more than enough for me."

Epilogue

"YOU KNOW, this is going to keep happening if you don't watch out."

"Can't a man carry his bride over the threshold? At least while he still has the strength?"

"Jason, no one is questioning your athletic prowess. It's just that if you insist on doing the manly thing, either we're going to have to raise the doorway or train you to look before you leap."

Jason rested his sore forehead against Claire's. "After the fortune I just spent renovating this place, I guess I'll have to be the one to adapt." He stepped back from the front door of the farmhouse and gently lowered Claire to the ground. "How about we crawl over the threshold together?"

"I can deal with that." She laughed. She pulled up the hem of her raspberry-colored shift and kicked off her sling-backs. In deference to her mother, she wore matching shoes for the wedding. They'd been married in a small ceremony in Grantham. They planned to take a honeymoon, trekking through some of the incredible places she'd visited with her father as a child and later as a news photographer, but that would have to wait until late summer. Jason was tied up with play-offs, and they were hoping that Larry would be able to collect on his twenty-dollar bet.

Simone, who had been elected mayor earlier that

spring, had officiated at the civil ceremony. Frankly, Claire and Jason didn't think she would have let anyone else do it.

Jason's mother attended, along with Claire's mother and stepfather. Naturally, Ted, Larry and Trish were there. Vernon, as well. He and Trish hadn't yet set the date, nor were either one of them willing to give up their condos. And their relationship seemed at times to be more dueling cell phones than anything else. Still, there was that dopey look in their eyes when they looked at each other.

Claire recognized that look. It was the one that appeared on her lips involuntarily all during the day—when she woke in the morning next to the man of her dreams—and of her reality. But she didn't have to be with him to get that look. Sometimes it popped up when she took the train into work. Or when she was munching on a tuna on whole wheat with bean sprouts and avocado. Or when she looked down at her hands and could imagine the touch of his on hers. Gentle. Strong. And just for her.

And she knew she was smiling that idiotic smile now as she got down on all fours. "C'mon." She turned to him. "Your turn now."

Jason laughed and lowered himself to the ground. "Oh, no, Leica. Don't get any ideas."

Claire looked around. The Akita—yes, that Akita— was eyeing them suspiciously and standing dangerously close to Jason's leg.

Claire laughed. "Don't worry, dear. I think he's more interested in the old brass water bowl that the professor left as a house gift." She started to move forward and heard something that sounded as though someone had turned on the hose to water the garden.

"I guess I was wrong," Claire said.

Jason muttered an oath under his breath.

And that's when she knew she was really home.

HARLEQUIN® *Blaze*™

Bestselling author Tori Carrington
delves into the very *private*
lives of two *public* defenders, in:

LEGAL BRIEFS

Don't miss:

#65 FIRE AND ICE
December 2002
&
#73 GOING TOO FAR
February 2003

Come feel the heat!

**Available wherever
Harlequin books are sold.**

HARLEQUIN®
Makes any time special®

$ **Saving Money** $
Has Never Been
This Easy!

**Just fill out and send in this form from any
October, November and December 2002 books
and we will send you a coupon booklet worth a
total savings of $20.00 off future purchases of
Harlequin and Silhouette books in 2003.**

Yes! It's that easy!

I accept your incredible offer!
Please send me a coupon booklet:

Name (PLEASE PRINT)

Address   Apt. #

City   State/Prov.   Zip/Postal Code

**In a typical month, how many
Harlequin and Silhouette novels do you read?**

❏ **0-2**   ❏ **3+**

097KJKDNC7   097KJKDNDP

Please send this form to:
In the U.S.: Harlequin Books, P.O. Box 9071, Buffalo, NY 14269-9071
In Canada: Harlequin Books, P.O. Box 609, Fort Erie, Ontario L2A 5X3

Allow 4-6 weeks for delivery. Limit one coupon booklet per household. Must be
postmarked no later than January 15, 2003.

HARLEQUIN® Blaze™

From:	**Erin Thatcher**
To:	**Samantha Tyler;**
	Tess Norton
Subject:	**Men To Do**

Ladies, I'm talking about a hot fling with
the type of man no girl in her right mind
would settle down with. You know, a man to
do before we say "I do." What do you think?
Couldn't we use an uncomplicated sexfest?
Why let men corner the market on fun when
we girls have the same urges and needs?
I've already picked mine out….

**Don't miss the steamy new Men To Do miniseries
from bestselling Blaze authors!**

THE SWEETEST TABOO by Alison Kent
December 2002

A DASH OF TEMPTATION by Jo Leigh
January 2003

A TASTE OF FANTASY by Isabel Sharpe
February 2003

Available wherever Harlequin books are sold.

HARLEQUIN®
Makes any time special®